CW00868453

ISBN-13: 9781071177617

Independently published

Available on Amazon.co.uk

'MY CLASSIC BOAT' - HOW WE CAN BUILD ONE

This is my clipper
I am the skipper
This is my masterpiece
I am the mouthpiece
I voice my past
That will last
Like the crow
Of Jack Sparrow.

CHAPTER 1

While living on the small Island of Mauritius, I have always been fascinated by the sea. You can call me a buccaneer if you like because of my obsession with pirate ships! But I am no pirate. Neither do I condone piracy. I have never been a sailor nor a seafarer. But I have been on a ship, travelling, and crossing countries in the 50's, before the aeroplane took over the sea transport.

As my Island is small, it didn't take me long to travel to the seaside when growing up, to watch all the ships on their journey to different shores. And I had always wanted to build a miniature ship to start with. I used to vandalize the bamboo hedges round the neighbourhood houses to find the right bamboo to construct a model. The pen knife in my pocket always came very handy then. With the knife, the long thin green bamboo would be cut to size, filed into strips and assembled into a boat shape, using strings to work my way in between the strips. Once completed, I took it to the sea whenever time was available to see if it could float. Sometimes it did, sometimes it didn't. But the concept of model boat building stayed with me and didn't materialise until late in life. It seems that after my retirement, as a psychiatric nurse, now in England, with plenty of time in hand, my childhood dreams started to rekindle with renewed vitality, despite the fact that I live far from the sea now!

The sea is a great mystery for me, just like the sun. The cold saline water, where does it all come from, nobody knows. Science always tells us a different story. Religion tells us another. A sailor will have his own version. But for a passenger aboard any of those classics a couple of centuries ago, venturing out, and crossing the ocean with full sails, challenging both enemy ships, and the high waves, would be like going through an infinite hell! It must have been awe-inspiring for anybody travelling in those difficult times, which was the only way to cross the ocean.

The sea is just an extension of the land but covered with salt water, sands and big black rocks. Very deep in some places, could be treacherous, and calm in another.

The perception of the ocean can distort your overall imagination when you come to sail across it, where things can get complicated. This is why different ships designs may come into mind. They were all made with wood, where artisans would display their cutting-edge innovations to make an ideal classic piece. And they were made to traverse the ocean however challenging the journey!

In the olden days, woodlands were abundant as trees could be found everywhere. Oak and Teak, Elm, Cedar were the main source of materials used. And because of their malleability when being exposed to hot steam, they can bend appropriately into shapes. They could float easily, and be diligently transported across lands and seas. At the dockyard, they were manipulated in such a way to make them last by the application of grease and fat during boat construction.

I am not going to show you or ask anybody to build a big wooden ship. Only a small classic model will do. You can follow me as I go along constructing one. If you think you can build a bigger version instead, well, good luck! But it is advisable to try a model one first in order to know what it takes, and what it entails. I can assure you it would be a big feat of achievement in attempting something to be proud of, something that you can leave for posterity. Just imagine a model classic, a typical work of art stood proud on your mantelpiece, with your signature engraved, or written somewhere on it!

In full view, not necessarily on your mantelpiece though, you can admire your workmanship daily, dote upon it, and let yourself be carried away on it by sea across the vast ocean of high waves, with all the perils lurking in the deep. I am no faint hearted after looking at my own model now, thinking what it would take to be the skipper aboard such a vessel. How to steer that bigger version amidst a bunch of rabble for crew, where decisions need to be made on a daily basis, who would obtain the lash, and who would walk the plank! How sad it would be to lose a member of the crew to the gaping sea, when justice was deemed unfairly carried out, where in some cases the skipper too could be next in line for the plank!

A lot of stories associated with pirate ships in the past. Most members of the crew were well - known rowdy ruffians. They were good with their swords, and ready to fight for the slightest of excuses. The sea was the only route they knew about how to navigate hither and thither, and how to get to their destinations. The ships for them were their world. The laws at sea would be the only ones existed.

With all these in mind, we must plan a good layout on the model ship deck. We must think of the amenities required by the crew to facilitate their stay for long journeys. There will be lots of ideas about fitted furniture on board. They will probably navigate in your mind endlessly, about how to get them, and where. Things like steering wheel, ladders, benches, steps and sails and cannons are hard to find on line. Even if you can buy them, they won't be the appropriate sizes to fit in particular spaces on the deck. In this case you will have to make them yourself, with pieces of wood of course!

Another thing is the rigging. While constructing a model we must bear in mind what sort of rigging can best be fitted to the boat. And what sort of sails do we need to make it looking good and sailable. The main rigging and the sails must produce an impact too, so that when you look at it, everything welcomes you on board.

WOOD - WHAT SORT?

As mentioned above oak is one of the best materials to be used. Other soft wood can also serve the same purpose, but has to be treated thoroughly as it is liable to become brittle with age. Oak can be preserved too, and that will make it last a little longer. As it is hard and durable, it is something worth having for building any masterpieces. It can be easily available in any D.I.Y shop, or unless you grow the tree in your back garden! But your local wood yard will always come to your rescue if you struggle to find the wood you want. The wood then can be planed and cut to size, the way you want it. Any additional work, such as carving, trimming, and filing to custom size, I am afraid you will have to do that yourself.

The bits and pieces of wood don't cost much. In the wood yard near where I live for instance, I can get them free, so long as I place a few pennies as donations in the dog's Welfare Box. Whenever I go for some I normally take a big bundle, because every little piece of wood count when you start building. Another reason for the big bundle is to save the woods from being burnt by the workmen at the yard, as customers hardly find any use for them, except people like you and me!

TYPE OF BOAT YOU WANT TO BUILD

Before starting you will probably have a few images of a clipper in your head. The most classical, with elaborate intricate details will no doubt come to your imagination. You will see them in all shapes and sizes, varnish or plain, with white sails and matching riggings. To cherish those images is one thing, to transform them into a work of art is another. If you are prepared to take a chance in performing your great masterpiece as you feel inspired, it demands more than a constant labour of love and enthusiasm. This is probably the reason many keen craftsmen misunderstand the patience and persistence involved. They suddenly feel they are not-up-to- it before they even get started. The more they think of the beautiful object of their imagination, the more they think of the details which they believe are unachievable, so disappointment takes over, with a feeling of hopelessness, and down tools!

Instead of getting your own wood, and designing your own clipper, you will no doubt find the easier way out. I mean buying your own kit. True there are many good models around which you can buy from reputable companies in the shop or on line. They may look as professional as they can be when completed. But they are not as easy to assemble. In fact they can be more tedious than building your own and can be costly too. If you can get your own wood, which cost next to nothing, manipulate it the way you want it to fit a particular model, your patience will grow despite the time it takes. And you can save money too if anything goes wrong. As with the actual kit, once a piece is missing or spoilt, it will be difficult to replace. In some cases, very awkward to get the exact fit!

You must remember too that you can't build a boat in a day. The Romans tried to do just that but found it hard to even build Rome! It takes time to make a beginning. It all depends upon how much time you have in your hand. All hobbies demand time and perseverance, but we must be aware too that we must prioritize other things around us, otherwise to stay with it for long period will likely cause some form of irritation from those around especially with bits and pieces of wood being thrown all over the place! I don't know if you have got a shed, or workshop to construct your masterpiece, if you do have them, it's an ideal place to do your work there. Otherwise the solid floor of a breakfast room, with a big table will do, because the pieces of wood can be easily removed with a brush then. Otherwise any carpeted floor will aggravate the problem as the woods won't get off that easily despite repeated hoovering!

I normally did my work in my breakfast room. Despite the solid floor, and my cleaning up afterwards, my wife always finds something to moan about, but pleasant with it though: I can say as she is kind and understanding!

CHAPTER 2

I have said hard wood is ideal to build a model, but it's better to make a start with soft wood. It can be treated later. This is what I am going to use as we go along.

So, get ready for the wood yard! Once you are there for your bundle of odd wood pieces, get a piece of pine. It will have to be long enough, say about 45cm long, and wide enough for your model specification and the right length you want it, with the width between 13 to 15 cm, and height about 1.5cm The height of the wood is essential here, as it forms part of the keel to be used at the bottom of the boat. The keel is the section at the bottom that will stay submerge in the water as the boat glides. It is deliberately made in this way to steady the boat. It can be filed, or thin down, for it to cut through its way in the ocean waves. You don't have to try it in water just yet!

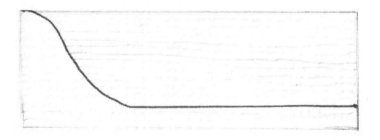

Fig 1

When you are in your workshop or whatever, cut your piece of pine wood the correct length you want your model to be. It is wise to have a template made to obtain the right front contour with thick paper or cardboard. Place the template on the wood and draw across with a pencil until the contour is visible enough as shown in Fig.1. Correct any deformed pencil mark with an Indian rubber. Once you are satisfied with the drawing, and the shape as appears, get ready to cut along with the use of your jigsaw.

I don't know whether you have used a jigsaw or a 'Dremel' tool set before, if you haven't, it is wise to try your hand at cutting a different piece of wood as sample first. Always wear your goggles and face mask when working with wood. Remember the blade of whichever tool you use will have to work its way round the shape you have drawn, therefore it will have to be thin and short. Position your wood on your table in such a way so that it will be made easy for you to work at. Start cutting the wood with the blade at right angle to give the wood a clean cut, and oil the blade cutter first if it is a bit sticky.

Once that piece is cut, consider sharpening the front edge of keel, only around the contour, as mentioned above, but do that only at quarter the length to make the front look like as if it's cutting through water when navigating. A small grain sandpaper can also be used here for the filing. The rest of the keel can be left alone so that it can rest snuggly on the stand which we are going to make later.

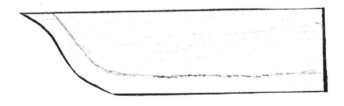

Fig.2

The next step is to draw another curve line about 3 to 4cm away from the edge of the keel, inside the length of the wood itself as shown in Fig. 2. This curve line must match the reverse side too. Another template made can be ideal for this work, and the line must be correct. I find it easier to use a drill with a thin bit to work my way along the line. The perforation will then appear on the other side in the exact position. Bear in mind that when drilling inside the curve, you will have to cut through it later to lodge the hull.

I think before you start cutting along the edge, it's better to build a stand to accommodate the boat itself. This can be done in measuring the length of the keel, by leaving enough space at the bottom as shown in Fig.3

Fig.3

To start with cut two pieces of wood about 2cm thick, with the right length. Sand paper them, or plane them. Get a flat piece wider than the two previous ones, but less in thickness about 1 cm, and glued them onto the flat piece, which again has to be a clean cut. Before being glued, make sure the keel rests loosely in the depth between the two pieces as shown in Fig.3, sliding easily, not tight fit, so that it can be removed as lots of work need to be done to the main keel.

Remember when working on any wooden craft, be prepared to get all your craft tools ready. Craft tools normally come in all shapes and sizes, and it all depends what you have got at home and how much are you prepared to pay to buy them. I personally don't have many as such, but I make use of any available D.I.Y gadgetry in my possession. The circular saw, jig saw, electric plane, drill, small hammer, wood chisel and a utility knife, with sharp blade, all these came very handy. What I normally do, I place all of them in one spot, so that I have no difficulty to locate them if wanted. This saves me time to look for them too.

To work with these tools can be daunting, often demands some skill of some sort. But don't be put off by it if you have never used them before, you will develop the skill as you go along. Always wear some kind of protection when working with the tools that you are not sure of! An emergency box with plaster and cotton wool can be a valuable equipment to be kept nearby too. I am not saying that you are accident prone, but you never know how these tools can be treacherous at times! From my own experience I inadvertently incurred a few small cuts to my fingers, but nothing serious to warrant an A&E!

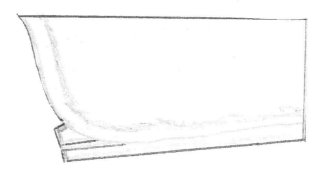

The wood with the designed keel, already in place will be the most important piece of the miniature boat. Indeed lots of work need to be done to it as mentioned before as we go along. Now is the time to cut through the line made on the keel previously drawn. With the utility knife, cut through that line while holding the knife at 45 degrees. Try to do it in such a way that the layer above the incision serves as a hook, when anything is placed inside the groove it won't come off that easily. Remember you can use a different craft tool to do the same job. The incision made underneath the layer will have to be a clean and tidy cut. It has to be done that way on the reverse side of the keel too, so that when completed, it can accommodate the hull, the body of the boat. It is better to finish one side first in this instance, to see how you get along. I know it's a pain's taking job that involves patience. But it has to be done in this way because the hull, which I will explain later how to fabricate, need to lodge inside the incision made with the knife. Once this is done place the keel inside the stand you have made to see if the line of incision is above the two pieces of wood of the stand as shown in the picture.

Now is the time to build the stern, which is the piece at the back of the boat. The wood used will preferably be between 1 and 1.5cm thick. And try to make the shape as simple as possible like the one shown. The simpler the shape initially, the easier it will be for you when you are ready to fix the hull. Remember the top of the stern will have to be exactly the same level as the top of the main keel when fixing it upright. A template drawn on paper will be ideal for this. Once the shape you like come up to expectation, draw the outline on the wood size of your choice, as mentioned, compatible with the correct size of stern to fit the boat you have in mind.

When ready, fix the stern to the body piece, using glue, nail or screw. The stern must be exactly in the middle of the body piece, reaching all the way down the bottom at the keel. In order to fix it properly and to keep it steady, I prefer to use both screw and glue. It is wise to use only one screw with an initial screw hole drilled into place first. What I normally do after I am sure that the stern is well positioned in the middle, is to apply glue onto the marked line in the middle. Leave it to set, then screw the stern to the keel in the screw hole initially there.

HOW TO MAKE THE DECK

The deck, as shown here, doesn't seem complicated as it looks. It has to be made in such a way that the back is about 5cm or 6cm 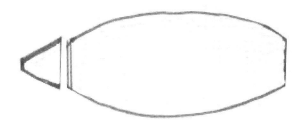 longer when it rests on top of the back stern. The wood size can be about 1 cm thick, and make to match the boat size. The length will have to be short at the front deck about '8 or 9cm' less, not reaching the front bit, because there will be an extra piece to come later to make up the full deck as it joins together. Or, if you are brave enough leave the deck all the way, make readjustment as you go along.

Again, a template is necessary here. Draw the top deck with the image of a coffin in mind, according to the length and size required. Polished the top well with small grain sand paper and rest it on top of the keel and stern, make sure it is in the middle, flush with anything underneath. Draw two lines, one opposite each other under the deck, using the board of the keel as a guide. Don't do anything to the deck yet. Once you are satisfied the way it looks, place it aside return to the keel board now.

Having already made a template of the stern, you can make two more templates now on similar lines. But one has to be smaller than the original stern, to go at the front. A second one for the back, will have to be a little bigger in size, and this to go near the 'back' stern. The two 'subsidiary' sterns, and the back one, will have to have tidy edges, so that the hull can go over them nicely later. When this done to your satisfaction, both 'sterns' will have to be divided in exact half in the middle, again with tidy cuts. A fine saw can be used, as a flat tidy edge is needed here because the two halves of the stern will have to be glued onto the keel board as they sandwich the keel on both sides as shown in the picture opposite.

When the glue is set, place the whole thing back on the stand. Don't allow the 'sterns' to touch the stand. If they do, they will have to be trimmed to leave a gap to accommodate the bottom hull later. Now place the deck back on top again. How does it look like? Is the deck well flush with the sterns underneath? Always be prepared with your utility knife, because there tend to be a chance that the 'sterns' will either be short at the deck or over, if you are doing it the first time. In this case an adjustment needs to be done to the 'sterns' or, the deck in some cases

With the deck sits very nicely on top, it is the time now to fix the deck not so firmly though, so that you will have no problem in removing it again when you are fixing the hull. To do this, look at the two parallel lines you draw previously underneath the deck. Place two dots with a pencil inside the space a distance from

each other. Have your drill ready to pierce two small holes in those dots that will appear on the other side, small enough for two little screws to drive through. The two holes on the other side will have to be tidied up and countersank. Place the deck back into place and get two little screws that will fit inside those holes, drive them through until flush with the top deck.

Place the whole 'skeleton' back on the stand, have a good look. Does the boat appear straight and well seated on the stand? If it does, don't glue it to the stand yet as there are some more works that need doing, such as to prepare it to accommodate the hull.

THE HULL

As mentioned before, the hull is the body of the boat. It won't be as difficult to construct as you imagine if you give yourself space, time and patience. I used pine wood as it can be treated after. Get as many strips of wood from a single block of 2cm width as possible. The wood yard by you may already have some off cuts ready to give away, or there to be 'condemned.' The length of

the strips must be at least about 70cm longer than the boat length to make it easy to plane.

While making the choice of wood to be used, don't forget to prepare a wider piece too, about 3 to 4cm width to be placed at the bottom of the keel, or use the same strips. You can use a harder piece for this one like oak, as that piece will be submerged under water 'in reality.' Now come the tricky bits: Try to plane the woods, so that it can easily bend round the curve of the boat, lodge over the sterns and inside the groove of the keel as shown in the picture.

To plane the wood strips can be tricky, but not difficult. If you've got a workshop, or a workbench it's fair enough, if you haven't, don't worry. I have got neither, but I use two chairs, where I place a hard piece of wood longer than the strips across between them. This will be my workbench whenever I got some wood to plane.

An electric plane is ideal for the job. Be careful when using it, as it can be treacherous. Remember to wear your goggles and mask for protection. If you have never used an electric plane before, it is advisable that you should try your hand on other pieces of wood first. When you are confident enough, try it out on one of the strips. Plane the strip at one go from one end to the other without stopping half way, otherwise the strip will snap and ruin everything. Do that again, depending on how thin you want your wood. Once this is done, go back to the 'skeleton.' It is wise to do the wider, bottom piece first as shown in the picture.

The wider piece which forms part of the hull must be fixed on both sides in exactly the same symmetry. Sharpen or file the edge of that piece as needed and prise it inside the groove, and place a tiny nail halfway at the back stern. Once both sides are initially fixed, with the curve touching the 'subsidiary sterns' as it should, place the skeleton on the stand again. Have a look to see whether it has come up to expectation. If it has, now is the time to apply wood glue. The wood glue you use will be a matter of your choice as there are lots of different brand in the market. Use a glue which is less thick, so that the overused can be wiped off easily.

Remove the whole boat, the 'skeleton,' from the stand. Take out the piece of hull from the keel, and the tiny nail. Smear glue inside the groove at the bottom all the way along the keel to the stern at the back. Now gently prise the bottom 'hull' inside the groove like before, not forgetting to place glue at the 'sterns' too. Leave it to set before you place everything back on the stand to have another look!

If everything appears good as it should be, this is the time to use the other 2cm strips of wood you have prepared. Take one strip at a time to work your way up from the bottom keel, and make sure it will bend easily across. File the edges if needed to make it fit the groove, and place glue inside the groove before fixing the strips inside one by one to form the right shape of the hull. The strips have to bend at the 'sterns' nicely, and touching them, otherwise there will be a gap which you don't want. They have to overlap with glue applied as required. It can be a little tricky to make the strips touch the previous ones as they overlapped. There so many ways that you can devise to make sure the strips stick. One of the ways I use is to get some small pegs. Place the pegs over each overlapping strips as shown in the picture. Leave it there for a while until being dried.

The final bit of each strip will have to touch the back stern. It is wise to leave it long at the stern because if it's longer, it can be made to stick to the stern by fixing a tiny nail halfway near the top so that it can be removed later when dry while trimming the stern, but be careful not to split the wood: this is why the strips have to be longer! The idea of placing the nail near the edge is to block the mark left by the nail as you are going to overlap the other piece(s) over the nail hole.

In working your way up with the strips, remember that all the strips must match symmetrically the other side up to the deck too, with the equal number of strips being used. They must make contact with the deck, without leaving a gap. The top edge of the final strip has to be flushed with the deck and glued to it.

After the hull has been done, nicely shaped accordingly, now is the time to complete the deck. Remember the missing bit cut short about '8 or 9cm, or so' in length at the front deck? Well, this must be filled now. That bit of the deck has to be designed in such a way with the right shape to cover the hull on both sides but lining the deck. To do just that, place the boat on the stand again. If you are pleased with what you see so far, design a template of the little missing piece of the deck, with the front pointed bit well 2cm thick over the front keel to make up the deck. This piece must be very neat, just like the long deck. Glue that on, and don't worry about the joint at the deck. There will be another piece of deck about 2cm thick and about 10cm long joining it on top of the deck. This should to be well designed having the same contour of the front deck. Once this piece is done, glue that one on too by joining the previous piece at the main deck.

How does the boat look like now? Again, if everything is to your satisfaction, you can proceed to the next level now: how to extend the last piece of hull over the deck. In order to proceed with this one, get a similar strip of hull, long enough to reach the length of the deck, but slightly thicker in height that has to bend round, shape easily at the contour of the deck. It has to fit at the edge of the deck, going well over the deck, as you don't want your seafarers to fall overboard, do you! If it doesn't bend easily near the front, don't worry. You can always stop it where it doesn't and make up another 'piece to fit' later. You can either glue the piece onto the edge or use some tiny thin nails or both in order to fix it. If you use little nail(s), make sure you drive the nail halfway, to make it easy to be taken out later, because once the piece of hull is firmly stuck together, you can take the nail out to prevent unsightly hole(s) in the hull. Place that piece of hull in the same fashion as on the other side of the boat. And where the two deck pieces reach, over the stern, you can join them now with another strip of wood at the rear deck.

Remember the 'piece of deck to fit' as mentioned above? Well make up another small piece of hull that can bend to join up together with the long strip already in place. It can be tricky when it goes over near the extended keel. If it is difficult to stick, apply a stronger glue, use a clamp, or, a string that can fasten both sides of the strip together. Once you are sure both sides are stuck, remove the clamp, or the string used.

CHAPTER 3

DECK FURNITURE AND OTHER ACCESSORIES.

At the front, well over the keel, where both sides of the hull and deck meet, there will be a small gap. You can either fill that up with another piece of 'hull' wood or leave the space open for those unfortunate souls who have to walk the plank!

Returning to the front deck where the thicker piece is elevated and glued, some form of balustrade, or railings must be constructed there for safety. Small wooden dowels can be used as columns for the balustrade; about four small dowels on both sides should be enough. Space out the holes to be drilled with pencil mark first at both edges. Drill through them, using the drill size of the dowels. But be careful not to damage the deck in the process. What I normally do is to use a smaller drill first for the holes before applying a bigger drill. Cut the dowels about 4 to

5cms long. Before placing them inside the holes, drill two or three tiny holes into them so that some thick white threads can go through like shown in the picture opposite. It is better to string all the dowels first before placing them inside the deck holes, where you may have to use some glue to steady the columns upright.

Now the elevated deck on both sides, front and back, is too high for easy access from the deck below. To counteract that problem, some form of walking steps need to be provided. If you can either provide step ladders, or small stairs which I am sure you can fabricate yourself by now, it will be a great asset! Otherwise I can assist you with these: To make the ladders you can use toothpicks and bamboo skewers as poles, which I am sure you can buy in any Supermarket! And there are so many ways of making them. To make the stairs you can use pieces of wood left out whilst making the hull.

To make a ladder remember you will have to make adjustment to the skewers and toothpicks. It is better to make a longer ladder, as the appropriate length required can be cut off, with the rest use somewhere else.

The toothpick should be cut into small pieces to make the 'steps.' They will have to be of equal length, well prepared by filing the end bits of the pieces, make it rather flat on one side to sit well on the skewers. The skewers need adjustment too where the 'steps' have to rest. Make the skewers flat a little on one end and use a utility knife all the time for these delicate jobs. And the steps have to be of equal distance to one another when wood glue is applied.

Another way of making the ladder is to bore small holes into the two main ladder poles by using a tiny drill bit. The holes will have to be the same distance on both sides. Use toothpicks again with exact length for the ladder steps, sharpen the end bits a little so that they can get inside the holes of the ladder poles.

THE STEERING WHEEL

To make a small steering wheel on a boat can be time consuming, and that demands patient with trial and error to contend with. This is why I presume you don't find many miniature classic boats with a steering boat. But the way I do mine can be very simple indeed. I normally get a small button which I find plenty in my wife sewing kit. The button has to be compatible with the size of your boat. Before choosing a button try to visualize how will it look like in the front of the elevated deck, where the steering wheel needs to be positioned.

If you are satisfied, smudge the button with a pine wood filler and leave it to dry. Once dried, sand paper it until smooth, keep the round shape of the wheel neat and tidy. Get a tiny drill bit, and drill in the middle until appeared on the other side.

The steering wheel on a boat is different from the one you find in a car, because it has spokes. To make the spokes, again use toothpicks. Cut the toothpicks the appropriate length when being viewed alongside the wheel. You will need eight of these small cut toothpicks to go round the wheel. The external ends (spokes) have to be rounded with a small grain sand paper, and make sure each spoke is equidistant from each other. At the centre, where all the ends of the spokes meet underneath the wheel, the ends have to be flattened so that they can be glued to the wheel. Make sure they don't go over the middle hole in the wheel, because a little nail or tack will have to be inserted inside this before being glued to the wheel staff, another piece of small dowel that will lodge by the elevated deck as shown in the picture below. I also have to emphasize that, whenever working with tiny pieces of wood, use tweezers to prevent the wood sticking to your fingers instead! Finally, to make the whole driving wheel look near authentic, you will have to use your own initiative there to achieve that aim. This is where the mystery of good artisanry comes into being!

The wooden anchor roller as shown, is fairly simple to make. Surely you will have plenty of spare pieces of wood left before being manipulated to make the hull. Use an adequate piece for that purpose. The shape the roller will take depends upon the image you have in mind, how compatible will it be when being viewed with your boat size. You probably have seen lots of pictures of rollers with chain round them, and anchors at the ends, hanging by pegs in the front of boats. But the image that will suit your boat again must come from you. A sample that comes up in my mind is the one shown.

Remember you need two pieces on both sides to make the roller-stand, join up in the middle with a short piece of dowel to accommodate the rolling chain. It is wise to get a longer piece of wood first to make the stand. Start drilling the holes in the wood to accommodate the middle dowel, using a smaller drill to start with. Then place the dowel over it to size it before drilling with a bigger size drill. Once the right hole is done, fix the small size dowel through. It is necessary to leave a bit of dowel well over one side of the roller to make a handle as shown in the picture. If it slides nicely, cut it to the length required, and cut both stands to the appropriate size too. Before placing the dowel back in, smear a little glue in the holes first to keep it steady.

You will need a small black chain to wrap round the dowel inside the anchor roller. I am not suggesting that you should make one because it is too elaborate a job to perform. But you can find some cheap ones in various charity or souvenir shop in your locality. And you may have to do some alteration to make it suitable for your anchor roller!

If you are satisfied with the anchor roller, wrap the black chain round it and glue the roller onto the deck at the front of the boat, where you find it conducive. Now you will need two anchors on both sides fastened to the chains. You can buy them in some of the boat shops, or on line, but if you can't find them, not to worry: You will have to fabricate them yourself!

HOW TO MAKE AN ANCHOR

To make an anchor for your boat is not difficult. All you need is a good imagination of the boat in question, and how the anchor will match your boat size. We don't need an anchor either too big or too small. Just picture your boat in your mind and try to figure out the exact size you need before you proceed.

You will need four flat nails for this venture: two nails for each anchor.

Take two flat nails with appropriate sizes and length and cut the square head off one of them with a pair of pliers, because you need it to be shorter. The bottom sharp bits must be used for the anchor, appropriately bent and shaped for them to hook below the surface of the sea. To bend the nails I use pliers, work my way in leaving the flat edge on the opposite side. To perform this task, I choose a hard surface, either a piece of hard wood, or concrete.

I place the sharp ends about 45 degrees upright on the hard surface, then prise the bottoms with pliers, bend them into anchor shapes. I hold them together, by placing each separate anchor with the flat side together, with one shorter than the other, because the longer nail head will have to have the black chain around it. Once satisfied with the look of them, I glue both the flat nails together, using hard glue. It will take sometimes before it's fully dried. Now the anchor on the other side has to be shaped and manipulated in the same way. Fix both anchors after being painted black with their respective chains using the nail heads of the anchor as hubs.

With the anchors fix to the chains, it is time to place it on the outside of the front deck, in an ideal position where the crew member can get at them in order to throw them overboard, thus stopping the boat. The side of the front edge will be sensitive in some cases, so be careful when working with it. The way I approach mine is to use a thin drill to pierce the holes on both sides of the front top deck first. I will then get two small black tacks and force them inside them. Once they are firmly lodge inside, I accommodate the chains by giving them two turns around the heads of the tack, leaving the anchors suspending.

CANNONS AND BALLS

To place cannons on pirate ships or boats depend upon the size of the vessels. Sometimes the cannons will be camouflaged. But wherever way you want your cannons on the deck, they will have to be appropriately designed, and pragmatic.

First decide how many cannons are required and place a pencil mark at the designated spot for them. To find the right cannons you will need a little improvisation. You can search some charity or antic shops, where you may more than likely find necklaces, string with small brown rounded beads either made from woods, or dry seeds. Along the chains you may find some small metal tubing strung in between the beads. You can use these as cannons, since they already got holes in them for the 'balls' to come out upon firing. See how many you need, then drill the appropriate size holes on the pencil mark you made on the boat previously, slide them in after glue is applied. Failing to find the right necklaces with the improvised cannons, I am afraid again, you will have to do it yourself.

To do the cannons, you can use the correct size dowels regarding your boat size. You can buy dowels at any D.I.Y. shops. Cut the dowels about .5 cm in length, and place a correct size holes in them for the 'balls' to come out. Smear some black paint inside the holes to give them authenticity. Once this is done, glue them to the designated spots by the deck.

Cannon balls will be too smalls to be visibly shown on the boats. To show them individually will take some doing. What I normally do is to construct a small trunk or get a small square piece of wood, and place it by the edge deck which can imply that it contains cannon balls. One or two trunks will be sufficient. Again it depends upon the amount of cannons you have.

PADDLING BOAT

A small paddling boat or lifeboat with two rowing paddles shown inside, stuck to the deck is a popular sight on classic models. On a big size version it is intended to take members of the crew ashore, as the water will be too shallow for the big boat. Or, to save members of the crew in high seas when they feel they are on their last legs! If you can design your own paddling boat, it will be a big asset, and very important indeed. It will not only give character to the boat, but enhance its authenticity, and display the skill of the model maker!

To fabricate the one I have in mind, remember there are other ways of doing them, you will need a small triangular shape piece of wood as a stern but remove the pointed bit a little towards end to make it flat. Get another lean piece that can easily bend for the hull. To bend the wood, you need the piece to be longer. Leave it for a while in boiling water until well soaked. Then hold the two ends together and bend it until a curve appears. Adjust the curve of the bends to the appropriate size of the lifeboat; don't worry if it snaps because you can always glue the ends together after being clamped.

Once the wood is bent to the appropriate size, tie the two sides together to make a V shape and leave it for a while in a warm place. If it's hot and sunny, you can leave it in the sun until dry, otherwise you can use other sources of heat. What I normally do with mine I place it in the oven on a low heat until dry, or if my radiator is hot enough during winter, I leave it on top. After a while, when well dry, the bend will stay in place. It is time now to cut the appropriate length you require for the lifeboat. Glue both sides of the hull to the stern using a clamp if possible. If you have difficulty with that, glue one side at a time until dry before starting on the other one and use clamp as necessary.

The front bit of the paddle boat can be left as it is if the bend is still intact. Otherwise, try an alternative, glue it: Get a piece of wood with the appropriate size, and cut it into a 'forward slash' shape to sandwich the two hulls joined up in the middle, then glue them together. You can use a small clamp in the process.

Once everything is dried, the bottom flat bit (keel) needs to be done. Place the open bottom bit of the lifeboat on a thin piece of wood. Make a pencil mark around it. Cut round that piece until you get the right shape. See if it will fit the bottom nicely. If it does, go back to the lifeboat, place a triangular thick piece to fit the inside front bit, lower than the boat edge. Get another piece to fit the back, and, in the middle place a middle piece for the rowers to sit down rowing. You can glue all the pieces to the boat now.

Once the lifeboat is completed, it's time now to do two small oars. To attempt this task, you will need two identical small poles about half inch shorter than the length of the lifeboat. You can use bamboo skewers found in Supermarket for that. Once the skewers have been cut to size, at the ends, glue a small flat piece of wood at the ends of each pole. Do they look like two small oars? If they do, glue them on top of the two ends of the boat, and paint the whole lifeboat when dried. But remember there are other ways of making a lifeboat, or a small paddling boat. The one I show you here is my way of attempting it.

CHAPTER 4

THE POOP DECK

The Poop Deck on a classical model boat is nothing like what you have in mind: Somewhere to evacuate, getting rid of bodily functions. Seafarers might well have used it in the past for that purpose, to be relieved, by squatting on the edge of the top deck in compromising positions. But such an act would be at their own perils when considering the raging sea down below, with possible hungry sharks navigating, awaiting the next prey, instead of the next dropping! However this deck actually means, 'punnis' in Latin, another word for stern, that lodge on top of the other stern below it. It is designed to obtain a better view really, especially for the Captain who could often be seen climbing the wooden stairs to reach the top. It was definitely his way then to keep an eye upon the bunch of rabble within his crew, as no doubt he had plenty to contend with. As we all know ship's captain of the past century were no angels, nor were members of the crew. Enormous consumptions of alcohol, lack sleep and food, no proper hygiene and sanitation, all these were enough to add to the toll of irritation and hostility. Aggression and fights did occur regularly. And Captains were forever known to dishing out punishments, as they were a law into themselves.

Just imagine navigating the high seas in the last century for months and ends, with no land in sight, no other folks around apart from the small unpredictable bunch on board. They all had to brave the menacingly, and merciless roaring high waves more often than not, and the fear of death couldn't be discounted that easy. We could visualize the psychological trauma on board through fear and lack of sleep, where hallucinations and delusions took over the lives of many. Understanding, respect and courtesy, were not in anybody's book then. This was probably what happened when Captain Bligh of the Bounty was on his journey back with his crew after visiting Tahiti along with the plants he collected. He was very ignorant of the nature of the mutiny on board. He mistook justifiable human problems for bad behaviours. He used his lashes on a few of his crew after tying them up to the stake, half naked, with gory body marks to bring home punishment that served as reminders. Some other poor souls were not so lucky though, as they had to walk the planks with their hands tied behind their backs while everybody anxiously watching. Captain Bligh seemed to enjoy the perverted spectacle then, as he never ceased to comment with his usual sarcasm: 'Be careful Sir you don't hurt yourself going down!' At least we could say that he was caring and had shown great respect by calling them 'Sir' on their last journey!

The Poop Deck wasn't an ordinary deck in the olden days. Apart from the equipment at the top, inside there were various furniture, such as cooking facilities, tables and chairs, with sleeping areas. The captain would have an office down there to keep an eye on things. But on a classical model it will be hard to show all these. All we can do is just imagine that they exist, make the deck plausible enough to visualise inside.

To construct the deck, you will need a piece of wood around 1 to 3cm thick. Take a measurement of the whole deck, then half it. Have a look at the other half towards the rear section, then half that again. Make a template of the Poop Deck starting anywhere by that half, and ending above the stern, as shown in the picture. Use the jigsaw carefully when cutting that small but thick piece from the woodblock, as it can be treacherous.

On top of the deck there will have to be an edge, or safety barrier, to prevent seafarers accidentally going overboard. The architectural design doesn't have to be elaborate. A simple barrier with small openings all along will do. Of course you may come up with other ideas. To do the small openings on the edges as windows, as shown is my way of doing it. Again it will be a delicate job, be careful with using a utility knife. When this is completed, glue another lean piece of wood on top above the openings. After the deck edges are completed, glue them on the deck, and glue the whole Poop Deck to the main deck.

Once everything is set, how about painting the whole boat then? To do that you can either use clear vanish, or an antic pine gloss. The latter is more appropriate, it is what I tend to use to give it an authentic appearance.

Now to go up the Poop Deck from the main deck, you will need a set of stairs. And another one is needed on the other side on top of the main stern to go down.

MAKING STAIRS

There are two types of stairs you can make. The first one is a ladder like steps fabricated with a flat piece of plank. To make it measure the distance between the main deck and the Poop Deck. Then get the plank with the adequate length very tidily trimmed to see how many steps you require, by making marks with pencil, where the horizontal pieces of woods need to go. To make the climbing steps, remember a convenient position is needed here as you don't want the stairs to be too upright, that can make it hazardous when climbing.

The other stairs that you can make is just like an ordinary one you may find in a supermarket, or anywhere in the house, but in miniature! To build one, get some little flat pieces of wood, stack them up appropriately, and glue them together accordingly to the required height. It is wise to paint the stairs before being glued to the boat.

DECKHOUSE OR CABIN

On top of the Poop Deck, a deckhouse or cabin can be constructed there. Inside which there will be the Captain office, with furniture such as a table with chairs, and various navigating artefacts. There might well be stairs leading to the deck below, where there will be sleeping areas, with dining tables and bunk beds.

Again, on a model classic boat it is impossible to show all these. However, we can always assume that they are there. The best we can show is the deckhouse itself, with windows and doors on the outside. It must be constructed with wood and has to be compatible with the boat and deck size, with the right height. A flat roof will be ideal for this.

To construct the deckhouse, use the same type of wood as for the hull. Try to obtain the right length with matching wood. Trim them and square them to make the exact fit for walls and roof. The roof needs be a little over where you have planned to make a door. You can glue the woods to the deck as you go along. The door may be half circular at the top, with a tiny knob made with a tiny piece of toothpick, and the door must be glued at the front, as shown in the picture. The whole house needs to be painted too.

THE RUDDER

A rudder is very important to a ship. Just imagine a ship without a rudder: It will be like a lifeless creature lost in a trouble ocean! A rudder can take many shapes. The one for your boat will obviously be of wood. And it isn't difficult to make. You can use the same type of wood you use for the hull, but thicker in size. The shape it will take is dependent upon your boat size. A template of the one you have in mind will have to be made first. Bring the template close to the rear, and see how it will look like. If you are satisfied with it, cut it out using your utility knife, and glue it at the rear in the middle of the stern, and the top bit underneath the deck. Be careful of the delicate job involved!

RUDDER STEERING MECHANISM

A manual wooden steering mechanism used for the rudder is normally placed on the top deck on any classic boat. You can easily find it when looking at a classic boat towards the rear. It is a pole structure with a tiller look, just on the top deck, where it is sandwiched with the deck and the rudder at the bottom. This mechanism is here to guide direction and facilitate movement of the boat. It should be operated by a helmsman or coxswain who knows his job; otherwise the boat will be all over the ocean waves!

To make the rudder steering mechanism, choose a dowel which is appropriate to the size of your boat. You don't need a structure bigger than the size of your rudder! The way I do mine is very simple. After the choice of my dowel size, I tidy it up by rounded the top with sandpaper, cut the right length I need, and drill a tiny hole near the rounded bit for the 'tiller' handle to go inside, as shown in the picture. You can use toothpick cut to size for this one. You can round the toothpick at the end too with small grain sandpaper. Once this is done, it needs to be painted before being glued to the top deck, just underneath where the rudder is situated.

Before I proceed to the next level about the mast and sails, I would like to point out that there so many other details that can be added to the top deck of the boat. In terms of furniture, you can add some long benches, stools, and balustrade next to the stairs. Remember everything needs be done in wood, glued to the deck and painted.

Balustrade by the stairs can be tricky but can be done. It will be very time consuming indeed. If you can do that I will raise my hat to you!

CHAPTER 5

MASTS, SAILS, RIGGING AND ROPE LADDERS

MAST

As you may be aware, all masts come in different designs. Anybody looks at a ship without sails, will probably find erected poles, standing upright and tall, with the ship not moving at all, as they are at the shallow ends. Some of the masts may well have been removed for repair, because they need regular attention, such as checking for rots due to birds' droppings! All of them have to be wood solid as they have to endure the strain of the wind on the sails with repetitive force.

The wood used for the mast is normally from oak tree, teak and mahogany, or any other hard wood. They should be trimmed to size to fit individual ship. They form various shapes with elaborate designs, for the sails need to withstand strong wind pressure. Likewise, on a model craft, it is no different, but the mast will consist of the long wood dowel being cut to size similar to the bigger versions as far as possible.

To make the topmast, you can get the wood from any D.I.Y shop. Have a look at different designs that you may have come across or try to become a brilliant trailblazer in making your own! You can follow my style too if you want, like I have shown in the picture.

Have the boat you have just completed in front of you. The amount of masts required depends upon the size of the boat and its positions on the topdeck. The length of the mast too is important. You don't have to follow the Viking longships mast, but simple ones will do! On the model that I made, I have used four long masts. And all of them are not of the same length though. You will find the first one at the front rather slanting, known as the Bowsprit, is shorter. The one, on the elevated deck at the front, is rather shorter still, and shorter than the two middle top deck ones. The one at the Poop Deck is again shorter. In fact, the only two on the middle deck are of the same length, longer than the rest.

Now, it all depends on the type of sails you have in mind, and how many are you going to use on each mast, as you may have to make some adjustment. By adjustment I mean placing some more props onto the mast call spars to accommodate the amount of sails.

On the boat I made, I used one sail for the Bowsprit, and another one at the Poop Deck with different design that takes a rectangular shape with the *spars*: Again I mean those pieces of wood that cross over the topmast. You will need two sails on each mast in the middle deck where the spars cross horizontally at the topmast. It is called 'topgallants' constructed with spars, as they are there to accommodate the sails. They should line up in symmetry with the others. The topgallants are made with different size dowel wood, cut to the right length, and fasten onto the masts as shown. Glue can be applied on the strings used for the fastening to steady the joint.

Once completed, have a look at the whole boat in front of you. See how everything appears to you. If satisfied, we can proceed to the next level.

SAILS

When looking at a boat, two images can come to mind: Either the boat is moving in the high seas, or at a slow pace until it stands still. You can see that by the way you shape and design the sails. Again, there are various designs you can dream of while making sails, but they all have to be practical and workable. The choice of the right linen fabrics will be an issue too. If you have a rag market near where you live, it will be an ideal place to look for them: this is where my wife found ours! The fabrics to look for will be a 'dirty' white colour and slightly thick when you feel it. Don't worry if you can't find the right colour, you can always dye it before you start with starch added to make it thick.

Having worked as a tailor with my dad when young, I know a thing or two about linen fabrics. I know how to manipulate them: I cut them to size, stretch them, toughen them, and sow them either by hand, or sewing machine. The sails I am going to show you how to make are the ones as shown in the picture.

To start with have a look at the Bowsprit. The only mast slanting forward, it contains one sail there. Assuming the linen fabric in your possession is the one you want, cut a piece slightly bigger than the size you want that will accommodate the spars of the Bowsprit. You notice that the sail curves in the middle, as if it is receiving the full blow of the wind. Well, it's because the boat is moving forward! So, the wind is pushing the boat with all the sails doing their jobs!

You may wonder how all the sails remain constantly curve on the boat to give it that feel it's moving! To put your mind at rest, I can say it is made that way by a simple trick of fabric manipulation. As mentioned before, starch is added to stiffen the fabric. When the fabric is dried, hard enough draw a pencil line about quarter of an inch from the edge inside across the four sides. Bend the edges along the pencil lines; bring them flat along the main fabric. You can use an electric iron for this job to make the pleats. Before you seal the edges (pleats) with glue, you will have to place a thin flexible wiring inside the pleats. You may find it hard to acquire the thin flexible wire. If no luck comes to you, after searching all the D.I.Y shops that you can imagine, I will tell you an alternative: Visit your garden centre! There, you are sure to find a flexible green wiring that gardeners tie their plants with. That wire is flexible enough, you can bend it whichever way you like, as it will stay into place afterwards. You can use the wire the way it is or peel the green rubber membrane before inserting it inside the pleats of the sails to be glued. Instead of using glue you can also sow the edges using a needle with invisible thread.

When all the pleats are dried and ready, now is the time to fix it to the Bowsprit. In order to fix it, bore four small holes in the four corners of the sail. Place four white thick strings long enough inside those holes. Before fastening them to the spars of the Bowsprit, bend the two sides into a curve in the middle that it will stay that way, if it doesn't, not to worry, it can be adjusted later.

The tying of the strings must be neat and tidy with small knots at the end. If the knots are a little rough, you can always place a little glue on it and leave to dry.

The other sails on the boat can be made in similar fashion. The two sails on each mast, or top gallants, have to bend appropriately in the middle as shown and fasten. Remember the sail at the Poop Deck is rectangular in shape, and this one will be taut, because it sways in the wind direction!

RIGGING

Rigging is an integral part of any sailing ship. They are systems that intertwine various features of ropes, and are accessory components that contribute to the versatility of their nature. The supports they offer to the topmasts, the topgallants and the spars are multifaceted. They can be used as ladders for climbing up to the sails to map the ocean at a height, and to counterbalance the ships in hazardous stormy weather.

Rigging have many designs that reflect the appropriate vessels. A classic model can be constructed to achieve equal ability with the same flair. To make small versions of the ideal rigging try to make one that is not complicated.

The way I did mine was to get some small black tacks, nail them while spacing them, opposite the four decks on the sides of the boat, but not the Bowsprit. Only three tacks per mast will do. You must be careful in nailing them, because the edges of the boat may get damaged and the split can cause you some headache. So the best way of doing it is to use the smallest drill to make the holes first before you drive the tacks inside.

When this is completed, find some medium size strings, dab them slightly with varnish. Once dried and taut, have an adequate length ready to work with. Even if the length you have in hand is not enough, not to worry, you can always add some more to it later.

Now you need some beads to the sails attached to make them more realistic. On a big size boat some of the attachments are made of iron or hard wood. It would be too difficult to make the same for a model boat. We have to resort to something similar, beads, as mentioned before. Charity shops, outdoor markets, or antic shops are ideal places you will be able to find them. They either come in small plastic bags, or chains in the form of rosary. In some of the chains you may find a few assorted ones with other trinkets of various colours decorating necklaces.

Most beads already have holes in them. You can string one or two in the rigging, as I said to make it more realistic, before you attach the rigging to the black tacks on the deck up to the topmast, or the spars. You don't have to use more Rigging than is necessary. Only three riggings per mast are adequate.

LATTICE RIGGING

This is another type of rigging which can add more character to the boat. The system of ropes is latticed like fishing net, where the crew member can use it like a ladder to climb up, dangle on it, and swings from end to end. To think about it can be difficult! But to make it, is a lot easier! I say this because when you think about the designs and the intricate details you have to go through, you can easily be put off from even attempting it. You may find what you have to go through, is beyond your reservoir of expertise. But the way I'll show you how I do mine can be a lot simpler.

With your boat standing in front of you, proud and elegant, measure the length of rigging required from the edge of the boat, where you want the rigging to start, up to the end at the mast. Assess the width of the rigging you have in mind. Once this is done, get a flat piece of wood longer and wider than the measured rigging. Drive a screw halfway near the top end of the flat piece of wood. That will be the only screw at the top, as you work your way to form a triangular shaped latticed rigging. Now have a long piece of the string, already dried with varnish, fasten it to the screw with two loops, while keeping the measurement intact. Bring the string all the way down to the right length as if you are making a triangle and drive another screw halfway down there. You will need two more or three screws (halfway) on the same lines, about 1.25 cm. apart, as shown in the picture. After stretching the first string to the bottom one, place two loops there, cut the string while leaving enough to fasten to the edge of the boat.

Get another varnished string about the same length as the first one. Fasten it with two loops to the screw again at the top like the one before, while extending the rest down to the second screw at the bottom, and do it like the previous one. Finally take another string (third one) and fasten it with two loops to the same screw at the top, and bring it down to the third screw, fasten with another two loops. Actually, what you have just done is an isosceles triangle with strings, with one straight string in the middle!

To do the lattice work, you will need some more of those strings smeared in varnish. When the strings are well dried and taut, cut them into small length, then glue them horizontally one by one, ladder- like fashion, to the strings of the triangular shaped Rigging, starting from the bottom. Try to reach the apex as far as possible.

When you finish with this one, do some more, to be placed opposite the mast where you think suitable. The longer the mast, the longer will be the Rigging, probably wider too. And whatever you do to one side of your boat has to be replicated on the other side.

ROPE LADDERS

Rope ladders can be done on similar line as the latticed rigging. Get a piece of flat wood like before, and with the same measurement. Drive two screws about halfway at the top, leaving a space of 2cm between them. Decide upon the length of the ladder required. Draw a straight pencil mark from the first screw (top of ladder) all the way down (bottom of the ladder). Drive another screw (halfway) there and place another screw halfway by it after a 2cm gap.

With all four screws in place, get two long strings thick enough to form the two main poles of the ladder. Place two loops of the string on the first screw at the top of the ladder, then straighten it all the way down to the bottom and place another two loops at the screw there. Cut the string, leaving enough behind. Now repeat the same on the other side, until the main two poles of the ladder look in good shape.

To make the ladder strings taut, smear some glue at the main poles and leave them to dry. Once dried, cut small length of thick strings longer than 2cm in length enough to form the steps of the ladder. Apply glue to them, then stick them one by one horizontally across the main poles, space them along the way. After they are dried, you can cut the odd bits at the poles with a pair of scissors. Thus, your rope ladder is done.

Rope ladder(s) on a ship is used in such a way that it can be hung on any part of the mast to help with climbing. So, on a model boat no need to glue it onto masts. Make it long enough so that it can just hang on the masts especially at the Poop deck, where an ordinary wooden ladder can not only be inconvenient but dangerous. The ladder can be left as it is in its natural colour state or painted with a clear pine varnish.

Now that your boat is ready with the appropriate varnish applied, and full sail for the ocean waves, be proud of your achievement. Like I said before, place her in a convenient place not necessarily your mantelpiece. Look at her now and again. If you have never been on this type of boat before, you can always dream to be the skipper, who both constructed her single-handedly, who steered her to many distant Islands on her journey. Even, if you don't know the way, I can promise you the boat will take you there!

46

TEARS OF A BUCCANEER

This is the story of how two pirates went to sea in the sixteen centuries to make a living. They had to plunder other vessels and battled their way in the high seas. The risk of survival was very slim when they had to travel an unknown journey. The fictionalised account here is about how they ventured out to plunder, and ended serving their country.

CHAPTER 1

It was 1587 both John Drumund and Francis Hopkins were in their own vessels travelling to Hispaniola, the hub for slave trade. It was a project financed by some members of the Elizabethan government of the time, to trade in slavery. There were five vessels altogether, belonging to the buccaneers. They had just been on an expedition from Sierra Leon collecting their slaves. Previous expeditions were a big success, so more ships were at their disposition now as there was more money to be made. They not only trade in slavery, but ready to plunder other Spanish ships for their gold and silver.

To reach their destination wasn't without any problems. It was their third voyage of that year. Phillip the second of Spain was already at loggerheads with England, and no doubt building up to a war. He had drawn new protocol for ships to navigate the seas, being well-aware of piracy that continually ravaged his ships, full of silver and gold. His new sea code gave Spanish galleons a monopoly over other ships and had also decided to end the illicit slave trade.

But John had to sell his wares. He would stand next to nothing to get what he wanted. As a notorious buccaneer he always found himself violated the Spanish monopoly. The Spaniards were appalled and furious, John had to use force on various occasions in order to dispose of his slaves in the main land. He plundered a few Spanish galleons and looted many to get as much silver and gold before refitting in the harbour for his homeward voyage.

However, John Drumund and his ships were unaware that the Spanish fleet was waiting for them at the harbour on one occasion. He had always considered the harbour to be a safe place for refitting. Surprised by the Spaniards, he had no choice but to fight. What followed was a fierce bloody battle with hand to hand combats, cutting down many with their swords and cutlasses. He had lost three ships out of the five, all sunk. He managed to move away fast from the scene of battle, with no knowledge of Francis whereabouts. He had lost most of his crew, and there were many casualties aboard his vessel. But he came out safe.

Meanwhile, Francis had no idea what had happened to his cousin John Drumund either, as his own ship moved away into the rough sea. John couldn't possibly have survived the ferocious fighting that went on, he speculated. Francis had a good look aboard his vessel: most of his colleagues were dead. He had to bury some of his best friends at sea. He was overtaken with grief but couldn't hide his emotions. He dropped a tear or two, and had to set sail home, navigating the harsh and cruel sea. It wasn't uncommon to see an emotional buccaneer, but the way he felt could signal the end of his seafaring life too.

He reached Plymouth Sound at last. Dusk was settling very fast. His ship badly needed attention so did his colleagues with fatal injuries. Everyone desperately needed food and drinks.

He quickly anchored his ship and asked for help to carry the wounded ashore for treatment. He was sad again for those that didn't make it.

He went to The Old Boar Inn for a drink and a bite. The Inn was full of unruly sailors, mostly drunken pirates. They all looked at him with suspicion, as they had never seen him before, with long beard, also got a patch over one eye because of injury he sustained. He had been at sea a few a month, unrecognised by those who knew him well before. But being so exhausted he couldn't be bothered to familiarize himself with the rabble. He took his drink with some grubs to eat and went to sit in a corner, trying to get the warmth by the open fire, while some drunken lasses scantily dressed at the top, interacting wantonly with those around. They were good time slappers, whose businesses were just as noble as those who went to sea to seek fortunes! But the sea for them was The Old Boar Inn where often bitter quarrels occurred to get a good 'trade'.

One of the girls approached Francis who was half asleep, with beer mug in her hand:

'Hello mister, do you want a 'boat'?' she asked, obviously talking in riddle.

'Boat, what boat? Talk no further lassy, go away,'

'I can see you want to sleep. I can fix you up you know.'

'How much then?' asked Francis.

'You look like a gentleman to me, one shilling for the favour.'

Francis walked away with her, despite his rough appearance and exhaustion. Halfway by the door somebody shouted:

'Hoy, lay off her, she is mine,'

'But you aren't mine, Clumsy,' the girl replied.

They continued walking outside, taking no notice. But Clumsy came out after them with his sword drawn. He could barely stand still being very drunk. He pointed the sword at Francis, while pushing the woman on to one side.

'Draw Sir, she is my wench,' he said.

Although ragged looking, Francis was tall and athletic. He could easily dispatch him, but dragged his heel, waiting for the man's next move. Another man suddenly came out with a lantern in his hand, wanted to see what was going on. He stood to watch and tried to stop the brawl. But the man with the sword became difficult. He wouldn't listen. He started lashing out at anything with his sword. The man with the lantern gave it to Francis to hold. He managed to get behind the perpetrator, who continued lashing out fiercely. He held him by his neck and stabbed him dead. A small group was watching. Francis suddenly showed the light on the assassin face. He was thrilled at what he saw:

'John, John,' said Francis.

Francis had found his cousin again, after thinking he was dead. The two of them went to the Inn to have a drink, while the body was seen to, and the Sheriff was called.

The Sheriff soon arrived on his coach, accompanied by a judge. There was enough proof as it seemed from those around to see what happened. Everybody vouched for John Drumund, and he had no problem in claiming self- defence.

Both men sat down afterwards with their beer, telling each other of their horrifying escapades at sea, how they managed to reach Plymouth with their wounded men on board.

John Drumund was tall, heavy- built, and accumulating his wealth through the notorious transactions in trading humans. These days we may regard the slave trade with abhorrence. But in the sixteenth century, the prevalent mind-set was blurred by prevailing cultural dogma. The church run peoples' life and not many were free to express views like today where our moral perceptions, were not shared by many. Slaves were regarded as expensive chattels to be bought and sold, where profits had to be made.

John was a well-known figure at the Inn because of his wealth and his sea adventures. Despite his rough justice at sea, many relied upon him for keeping them employed. He was a close associate member of parliament, and his trade was a good source of revenue. He was encouraged in what he did if it meant plundering the Spanish navy. His venture in the Spanish Main was lauded like many others pursuing the same trade, especially as Spain was going to send the Armada to fight England.

'When you left me outside the harbour to go your own way that day, I thought I was a gonner. I had to fight my way, ran back quickly, trying to cling on to the top rigging of *The Conqueror*, out of sight, with my cutlass, watching my men down below fighting it out. None survived the Spanish morons. They left after searching the vessel for gold, but I already hide it at the harbour with the assistance of a crew member. I saw one of the cannons hit the main hull, it shook the vessel, only moved it forward instead. They tried to sink the whole thing with more cannons, but I quickly disengaged the top sails in the wind directions and moved northward. They gave me a chase, but I was too fast for them.'

'Did you find your way northward then, I heard there is no passage there as it's very rough. How did you manage to find your way?' asked Francis.

'I lose them in the thick fog and steered my way downwards. The waves were too high.'

'You said you hide your gold? Do you still remember where?'

'I surely do…. we need to go there together. Her Majesty will have to pay for the journey. I've lost money and men you know. I have only two ships left, yours and mine. It will be some time now before I go again for the long journey. How is your ship, not badly done, I hope? Anyway, I've got a new job, at the dockyard. I will repair both, do small jobs before taking on Spain again.'

'Mine is badly shaken too. The rudder is hanging by the skin of its teeth, with a hole in the stern. I only just managed to get here in fooling the morons into thinking we were all dead. I think I had enough of the sea John. The sea ventures make me weep. When thinking about the men I lost, and who I had to throw overboard, it began to pain me.'

'This is the life of a buccaneer my friend. The sea is where we belong, you have to live and die in it. No room for sentimentality when your own life is threatened. Those who die at sea are real heroes, enemies who fought them are the throes in the bums just like the cruel seas, other buccaneers, the morons, and your own conscience.'

'Our own conscience, this is what we have to battle with! Killing, Killing, do you ever have regrets when killing another human, like the one you have just done? I know it was a legitimate kill, but deep inside you must feel for it.'

'I always do. But beware; what the Good Book says is different. You can't love your enemy and turned the other cheek if he is going to kill you. Nothing is said about the savages and slaves. They look like us but different. They have no souls like us because they don't go to church. They are made to be unpaid servants to serve us. Members of Her Majesty's think it's not proper to talk well of them.'

'And what happened to those who talk well of them?

'I heard some of them are being persecuted. They are considered unorthodox and heretics.'

'I have my own feelings regarding treatments of others. I am no churchgoer, but I've got my free thinking, that, nobody can take away. What I think is wrong, I can feel it inside. Religion plays no part. Religious sermons that attend to no mind and soul are like preachers parroting to the high waves at sea, nothing is internalised. Bless those who can understand, think and feel.'

'If you have strong views regarding your beliefs, and you don't attend the church you must watch your step when you are not at sea. You will soon see them coming after you. I know you are soft towards slavery, and those who are worse off, but, no man of religion. When you are on land, you must abide by the church laws, with regular Sunday attendance. This is a Christian society, where biblical notions of subservience to the crown and the laws cannot be dodged. '

'If I live by the sea, who cares? I don't have to bow to beliefs of others. Hoping there will be somebody someday who can see the light. It will be bold of him. For now people are afraid to open their mouth. Religious doctrines are not being questioned. Bible teachings and interpretations are meted out only to some privilege few. Obviously, it will never occur to them to reform, if it means compromising their self-interest and fear for their lives.... are there any jobs at the dockyard that I can do?'

'You can join me at the yard. We are all preparing in building the best ships to fight Spain. We are being paid by Her Majesty the Queen. We have to win that war, otherwise Catholic Spain will take over, they will kill us and our Queen, and England will be in the doldrums.'

After the long chat both buccaneers decided to settle down for the night on their own stricken vessels that were berthed not far from Plymouth coast. But with the unrest in the country because of Spain threats, they were advised by the coast guards to stay at the Inn.

CHAPTER 2

On the next day Francis was woken up by the early morning June sunshine, as reflected through the window cracks, whilst still in bed. Up he got, quickly opened the window. The commotion on the streets was new to him. Even the whole entourage was weird, after being away for so long. The streets were already infested with hawkers gesturing around with noisy shouts about the description of their wares. There were bread sellers with honey in them, carried on the backs of their donkeys. There were meat sellers and vegetable sellers. There were fire sellers, for those unfortunate enough to see their fires in the house extinguished, and there were even sales for private lingerie such as panties, even codpieces. But there were nothing for the women though, in terms of underwear. No knickers or bras because they were not invented then!

Through excitement Francis rushed downstairs to get washed and cleaned. On the way he grabbed a glass of ale at the counter as no tea was around either. He had to attend to that call of nature desperately. But no cesspit, he had to find somewhere somehow. The bushes and trees were the only safe spot for some means of privacy, especially as there were an abundance of mulleins to provide an excellent swipe at his behind!

On the way back he came across renewed disproportionate thrills on the streets. The flower girls were out with their baskets of various hues, fragrant and fresh, in contrast to the gong farmers who were carrying their heavy loads from cesspits of the night before! He saw a man pilloried, still walking around, with his head and hands held tight, showing red under the strain of the heavy stocks. He didn't know what he was guilty of, some said for horse stealing. Others said for sleeping with the woman next door!

However, the man could still talk after being fed bread with honey and ale by Francis. It had been a long time since he had such a treat. He gobbled what he had in no time, and stared at Francis with his wide eyes ready to pop out:

'Good of you Sire, I did nothing wrong, see where I am now. I was accused of being spying, not true,'

'What's your name Sir, I seem to have seen you before,' asked Francis.

'I am Coldicot, the coxswain of Captain Drummond. After coming out of sea, I got caught in a brawl. Two men grabbed me. That's him, that's him they said. The Sheriff was called. Instead of hanging me, they handed a lesser punishment, considering my plea of being no spy. I will be grateful to you, Sir, if you can get me out of here.'

'I remember you Sir…I am going to see the Captain, he can vouch for you. How long have you been in such a state? What can I do, I am new here myself,' said Francis?

'Since yesterday Sir, they left me like that. The town crier is coming soon with the Sheriff I heard, to deliver the Queen's message,' said Coldicot.

Francis was anxious to know what the Queen had to say about the impending war. He preferred to hang around for a while instead of heading to the dockyard yard to meet John as arranged. He could tell by the peasants arriving in the vicinity, a big crowd was expected, and he wouldn't hesitate to press on Coldicot's release with the Sheriff. The Country's need for any available rascals to fight the war was well known then. There might be a high reward for recidivists, who could show their inborn talents of villainy to defeat the enemy. For once there was some form of leniency for those to go above the law!

The crowd by The Boar Inn started to swell. The noisy chit-chats and murmurs within soon came to a standstill, as two men on horseback appeared. They were people from the State. They had come to appeal to the crowd's kind nature and invoke them with the deep sense of patriotism, to either fight or die. The message carrier was ready to deliver what was written on that wide scroll of paper. He held the message tight while still on his horseback, rolled it down from top to bottom. His job was only to hold it whilst a second man read it out through a cone shaped loudspeaker:

'Ohoy...Ohoy..,' he boomed.

'Important message from Her Majesty: I appeal to you, my devoted citizens. As a woman I am ready to take up arms myself to defend our country. But as you need me as Queen, I demand that your responsibility is just as mine to defend this kingdom of yours. Use whatever it takes to defend our honour, if you don't want Catholic Spain and Europe to take over England. Spanish spies are already in our midst, so beware, and deal with them accordingly. Long live England.'

After the short message, the crowd shouted, 'Long live the Queen,' and started to disperse. But somebody arrived jostling his way with the pillory around his neck. Francis was on his way to meet the officers, to request them to stop and consider Coldicot's case, as he was in desperate need for a fair trial. He was met by John Drummond on his way. He came to make the same request. Surprised to see John Drummund, known to be supercilious, Francis never thought he would meet him in person demanding for his worker's release. But John needed some more recruits now especially those who knew him well. He was planning to inflict some damages to the Spanish navy Armada in the last stage of its final construction before she set sail for England.

John recognised one of the officers on horseback, as he was seen in the House of Parliament on several occasions. He asked the officer:

'Sir, in what manner of demeanour my man was arrested and pilloried. He is one of my crew, well known around here,'

'He was recognised to be a spy Sir. We are waiting for evidence.'

'Recognised, that's absolute nonsense Sir. We all look like rascals. Does this make us all slaves, looters, and criminals not worth serving our country? I need man like him to fight war, as you can see by the weight he bears daily, he is genuinely a strong Englishman, ready to fight for his country,' replied John.

'Since he is your man, he will be released Sir. But remember there are many strangers here, everywhere, we don't know who is who. I trust your words Sir. The Sheriff will release him, he had the key. We are on our way to meet with him.'

The Sheriff arrived before long in his horse drawn coach. He was surprised to see John again defending this man in a quite different circumstance. He knew about John's affiliation with the House of Parliament, and that the government relied upon man like him to serve the country. Without getting into any more details, the key was given to release Coldicot.

Francis couldn't wait for Coldicot's release from the weight of the stocks on his shoulders. He went to attend to him in order to help him sustained his balance. But once released, Coldicot spread himself on the ground, passed out. There were blood red marks around his neck, and both wrists, and seemed weak on his feet. He had to be seen to by the apothecary. Both John and Francis decided to take him on horseback to the nearest one by the Inn despite the stench that bombarded them.

Caldicot's wounds were seen to by the physician whilst being placed on the floor. He came to at last, with the burning sensation of his skin sores, resulted from the remedy application. It was a concoction of pigs' liver, lard and mandragora. They were known remedy, reputable to cure all skins ailments, sores, bruises, and remained undisputed in the field of apothecary prevailed in those days. Coldicot recovered quickly but refused to stay at the Inn afterwards as arranged by his boss. He desperately wanted to go away in case of renewed accusation because of his appearance. He managed to leave the Inn overnight, and disappeared.

John Drummund was already working hard along with Francis trying to get his vessel prepared for an expected encounter with the Armada. They would try to do as much damage as possible to prevent it from sailing on time, while England was building its defences. After much persuasion Francis reluctantly accepted John's offer to stay at sea. Extra canons were fitted on board *The Conqueror* with firepower that could cause enough damages, more guns, even bows and arrows donated by peasants. A few more buccaneers were being employed whose assistance was immensely applauded. As dusk was approaching, everybody was tired, they laid down their tools. The ship was transformed into a doss house, with men sleeping in every occupied space.

Francis remained on guard that night while everybody slept. He went round the deck with his lantern, searching for any opportunist intruder, so called spy, who could come on board by stealth. He climbed up the Poop Deck, nothing there, all sleeping. He had a long look around holding the flickering lantern, and aimed at the glistening water down below. The sea was still calm. He stood there for a while, then he saw a subtle apparition approaching like a shadow nuanced by the semi lunar light. The lantern was held high, swinging from side to side. He could see a man now paddling towards the ship. The man waved, with both hands moving from side to side, trying to attract his attention that he was no enemy. Francis seemed to recognise him, he quickly ran to get the rope ladder. He met John who was woken up from his deep sleep. They both enfolded the ladder at the deck, and let it roll all the way down near the water edge.

The man was weak, and exhausted. He found it hard to climb up. All he could do was to hang on at the bottom of the ladder. He was obviously struggled in climbing as his steps slipped a few times on the rope ladder. Both John and Francis were watching him from the top deck. John boomed:

'Hoy…You stay there, we will pull you up.'

He hanged on to the ladder tight while he was pulled forcibly up by the two men, and as soon as he was near the deck he was assisted to come on board. The lantern was shown to his face: It was that Coldicot again.

'How did you manage to find us? I thought you were poorly. You were told to stay at the Inn,' asked John.

'I had to move out Sire before they came to get me. I don't trust people at the Inn.'

'Where did you get that boat?'

'I took it from the coast Sire.'

'You sure nobody saw you? Remember once you are here you can't get out. We are all watching the enemy and preparing for war.'

'Nobody saw me Sire. I've come back at the right moment as you are going tomorrow.'

Coldicot tried to take his place among the crew on board but found the distance apparent. He appeared better than expected, as if the punishment he endured previously had no impact on him. He was stocky, larger than both John and Francis in size but shorter, with a ginger beard, and hair pushed back. Rather coarse and brutish looking, typical of a common buccaneer, but his compassionate look could falsely disguise his true nature. It was that look on his face that melted Francis with the compassion echoed in the Bible: Jesus Christ was carrying the Cross, an absurd metaphor with Coldicot bearing the stocks!

He was among John's crew on their previous journey to Hispaniola, where the fight was severe and brutal on land and at sea. The Spanish fleet gained grounds then, as the pirates had to flee. During the fight Coldicot disappeared from the seen. He was thought dead, until John found him pilloried. His own colleagues refused to clear his identity when they found him in stocks, as they could be charged with being complicit. The Sheriff knew who he was, being alerted by Signor de Souza, a Spanish Colonel working on the Spanish coast to watch for English pirates. The Colonel had always tried to coax any English pirates by devious means to use them as decoys. As Coldicot vanished during the fight at the Harbour, it was the Colonel men who captured him. The Colonel was willing to use him instead of putting him to the sword. He took him back to Spain for his future voyage, because for any Spaniards to set foot on the English soil with no support could prove dangerous.

The Colonel and the Sheriff had known each other before because of their underhand motives. He would arrive with his Spanish galleon bearing an English flag visited Plymouth harbour during the night carrying some gold and silver for the Sheriff. Being both Catholic they had concocted a plot to make a Catholic uprising during the invasion of England. But as the fight with the pirates became too regular, his motives were divided. On one hand he desperately wanted the Sheriff to stop turning a blind eye to the pirates, ravaging the coast of Spain, on the other he wanted his money to be well spent in furthering his dark motives as advocated by Phillip the second of Spain.

He decided to use Coldicot as his henchman but remained a prisoner on board when travelling to England, with a promise of release and a handful of gold if successful.

The Colonel would normally come at night with another Spaniard called Pedro on board, who knew the Sheriff too. He had been instructed previously where to find him. Once berthed, both the Colonel and Pero would get out, used a life boat to go ashore to fetch the Sheriff. The Sheriff would then arrive with his coach on his secret mission to collect his bounty. But the Sheriff couldn't always be found by the Boars Inn where the rendezvous normally took place at a secret location.

CHAPTER 3

One night the Colonel arrived, accompanied by Pedro and Coldicot on board. He stayed on the main ship, whilst both Pedro and Coldicot went ashore. But the Sheriff wasn't present. He had gone to meet up with his associates. They were both stranded, as the Sheriff came back late. They soon found themselves accosted by the coast guards as they appeared suspicious. They stopped Coldicot in order to ask questions, whilst Pedro stood in the background. There was a struggle, Pedro suddenly panicked, took a shot at the guards, and killed one of them, then ran away in the dark towards the lifeboat. He rowed the boat near the ship belonging to the Sheriff. He remained there for a while hiding, until the coast was clear before he went back to look for Coldicot.

Coldicot wasn't hurt in the struggle but beaten up. The Sheriff was on his way back. After establishing Coldicot's identity which he already knew, the Sheriff refused to hang him as demanded by the villages. He was placed in the pillory instead for a slow death to set an example to others. But unknown to the villages, he didn't want to kill Coldicot as he could be of some use to him. When he found that he worked for John Drummonds, he was ready to release him hoping that Coldicot would meet up with the Colonel again for further transactions.

When being questioned by John Drummond on his arrival on board, Coldicot was held in deep suspicion, and everybody was wary. How did he know that *The Conqueror* was about to sail the next day? He surely knew a thing or two about what was going on in his vicinity that might well foreshadow future events. His lifeboat was constantly being watched. Instead of mingled with the crew as usual, he was kept as a prisoner. John and Francis were forever on the look-out for any goings on around *The Conqueror*. Towards dawn John decided to go down the rope ladder to have another look. What he saw was no surprise: the lifeboat had disappeared!

John quickly went up the ladder to question Coldicot again under duress now. He was tied to a pole on board the ship, stripped to his waist. John had a lash in his one hand which he used a few times, while the crew stood and watched. Even Francis who felt sorry for him previously, suddenly realized how mistaken he was. Coldicot was a liar, could be a spy too.

'Now you tell me the truth what went on, where did you get that boat? Who was travelling with you?' asked John.

'I know nothing Sire,' replied Coldicot, again and again while in agonizing pain.

John looked at Francis, who felt that they should postpone their venture late on the night until a future date. Somebody outside had known their plan and somebody from within had divulged it. That somebody outside would be hard to find if nothing would come out from Coldicot. Apart from knowing about *The Conqueror* 's departure that night, John suspected that Coldicot must have some rapport of some sort with some Spanish sailors, enough to alert Colonel de Souza about the ship's refitting in the harbour at Hispaniola during their last journey, where both John and Francis nearly lost their lives.

They again asked:

'Who was on board the lifeboat? Did you steal it from somebody?'

No answer from Coldicot. He could feel the repeated pain of the lashes marking his body, but his eyes were wide open with his head bowed in despair. He could hear his own agonizing cries and shouts, although saying nothing. John came up with another idea, known to be cruel, but could be effective if death was staring at him at the door of hell.

'If you don't want to tell us, then you will have to walk the plank. Get everything ready Captain Francis,' said John.

To hear about the plank was enough to put the fear of painful death in Coldicot. It would be like challenging the devil and the deep blue sea. He suddenly awoke from his ordeal and started to tell what he knew.

'I used to work for the Sheriff, as a goatherd, tending his horses too. I saw Colonel de Souza with him once, talking in Spanish, while walking in the stable. I hide behind the door as they walked around. The Sheriff suspected me, he asked me to attend the horses instead, to be out of their sight.'

'Go on, go on what happened next? 'asked John.

'I want to tell people about the Sheriff, nobody would believe me. No doubt the Sheriff would try to shut me up if I stay around. So, I left his employment to find a job at sea with you Captain Drummond.'

'Who is Colonel De Souza then?'

'I don't know Sire, it was his men that captured me, took me in Spain.'

'How did the Spanish know that we were refitting in the Harbour at the Hispaniola? And how did you know that we are sailing tonight?' asked both John and Francis in turn.

'Mr. Sheriff has spies everywhere. He knew when you fought with Spain at sea that you went to refit in the harbour.' Coldicot replied.

'And how did he know that, come on?' asked Captain Drummond.

'I heard Clumsy talk about it at The Inn Sir. I told Sheriff,' said Coldicot.

'And how did you know we are sailing tonight?' asked Francis.

'One of his spies told me, and he provided me with a lifeboat to join you before you go.'

'There was somebody in the boat with you isn't it?' asked Francis.

Coldicot went quiet. He then nodded in approval:

'Somebody was with me.'

John looked at Francis, both stunned. John couldn't believe it. He couldn't believe who to trust among his crew. The Sheriff certainly knew about every move of pirates that sailed from the coastline. But to find out how he knew would be a big denial on his part. The fact that he even provided a lifeboat to Coldicot with a man in it to rejoin *The Conqueror* was a bit of a twine which John had to unravel. Was the Sheriff and the Spanish in collusion? But how news got across after all at such a short notice? He then realized that it must be The Boars Inn, where pirates mostly meet, one of his crew must have inadvertently let the cat out of the bag when drunk. He was glad he killed Clumsy after all!

Leaving Coldicot still tied up, they moved towards the deck, away from everybody on board. They both realized that it would be a while now before they set sail again. They have done well in the first instance not to let anybody out of the ship to wander freely where secrets could be divulged. Although John didn't ask for the man's identity who accompanied Coldicot, he was keen to find out for himself. He knew Coldicot was the biggest liar, it could be a waste of time trying to get the truth out of him, but he had to try by all means possible!

Apparently when Coldicot arrived with Pedro to find the Sheriff that night, where one of the guards was shot dead, Pedro never went back to the mother ship. He was still around in hiding. He wanted to know what happened to Coldicot, in case he revealed all secrets to the authority. On the night that Coldicot was seen to by the apothecary and felt amazingly well after, Pedro was hiding in the background somewhere waiting for Coldicot to come out. He was ready to take him back to the mother ship and had his lifeboat on standby near the Sheriff ship. The Sheriff's men was around too, trying to find both Pedro and Coldicot. But Pedro in disguise, easily camouflaged with the guards by wearing the same hat and uniform, was quick to grab Coldicot as soon as he recovered. With a gun pointed at Coldicot, he led him for a long walk towards his lifeboat.

They rowed under the moonlight night, heading for the Spanish vessel disguised with an English flag. But the Spanish vessel wasn't there anymore. In the same vicinity was *The Conqueror* with a newly constructed Spanish maid figurehead at the front, which appeared convincing enough to be the same Spanish vessel. Coldicot was asked to wave as soon as he saw the light shining, with no knowledge who was on board. Both had a shock to find that it was the wrong vessel. Coldicot recognized Francis instantly. It was too late now to escape. Pedro had to hide underneath his large black cloak in a supine position to avoid detection, until time arrived for him to escape.

Pedro desperately wanted Coldicot alive, because apart from other underhand motives, he carried the secret where John Drummond hid his treasure in Hispaniola. He told Pedro about it when captured, but never revealed the spot. It was Pedro who suggested to Colonel De Souza to use Coldicot as a go-between with the Sheriff at Plymouth. Pedro's intention was, once on the Spanish soil in Hispaniola, he would take Coldicot at gunpoint to show him where the treasure was hidden without the Colonel's knowledge. But his entire plan hadn't worked out!

When he lost Coldicot, Pedro thought he had to make a move before dawn. He decided to move out stealthily as the coast was clear. He rowed along the coast, and by chance he met up with the Spanish Ship who was looking for him too. Colonel De Souza waved back at him. He was pleased to be in the right vessel this time but had some explanations to do!

He told Colonel De Souza what happened, how Coldicot ended up on the English vessel again. The Colonel wasn't pleased. He had wished Coldicot dead instead of somebody else. The fact that Coldicot was still alive presented a greater problem for the Sheriff especially.

'So why didn't you kill him and ran away when you have the opportunity? I didn't want him back here,' asked the Colonel.

'If I did that my own life would be at risk as the guards were around. When I killed one of the guards, I managed to take his cap and ran away. I went back to the Inn late after wearing the cap, when everybody was drunk. They didn't take much notice of me thinking I was one of them. I heard where he was as they were talking loud.'

'Where did you go afterwards? I am sure they would be looking for you.'

'I went to see the Sheriff. I stopped at his place, he gave me a uniform, but didn't see Coldicot. Sheriff said he was locked up. On the next day I saw him with a pillory. I again hide from him while he carried the 'thing' on his shoulder. I saw a man gave him drinks and food. I knew then he was going to be released, because the man looked like an official.'

'What happened when he was released? I thought the Sheriff would ask his men to get rid of him?'

'He did, but I don't want to be the one who did it. I wanted him back with us.'

'Can you recognise the ship he went on?'

'Yes Colonel, it was one like ours with a senorita at the front...'

'I know that ship. It belongs to the pirates. You will never capture him again now,'

CHAPTER 4

On board *The* Conqueror, Coldicot had let out the biggest secret: The Sheriff involvement with Spain. John was sure there was something fishy in the air. Acknowledging England was on the verge of war with Spain, the Sheriff was fraternising with a Spanish Colonel on English soil. This no doubt constituted a plot which the authority had to be informed. John and Francis determined to question Coldicot again as they realised, he was hiding something.

Still remained tied up, he was given a drink before another course of lashes started. Coldicot opened his eyes, looked exhausted, but well aware of his ordeal, and further chastisements.

'Remember Coldicot, walking the plank is another alternative unless you tell us more about the man accompanied you on the boat,' asked John.

With the lash in his hand ready to inflict more pain, John looked at Coldicot.

'His name is Pedro, Sire,'

'And who is Colonel De Souza?' asked John again.

'He is a Spanish general. He always comes to England to give gold to Sheriff. His ship has English flag.'

'Dou you know why he gave gold?'

'No Sire.'

'How did you come to his employment?'

'I met him in church, and he told me to come and work for him.'

'What church is it?'

'The Catholic Church.'

'Where is that Church then? '

'Inside Sheriff house Sire,'

To hear about both Coldicot and the Sheriff religious affiliation wasn't a good omen for the country. Catholic Spain had always been trying to have England converted to Catholicism in line with Europe. England was considered a heathen country because of her Protestantism. Many plots against her Majesty had been foiled before due to her excellent ministerial spy work. But John had to find out whether another uprising was brewing spearheaded by the Sheriff.

John and Francis walked towards the office in the Poop Deck and sat down, with the lash still in John's hand. They wanted to discuss what they had heard further.

'The Sheriff will be in dire trouble if the authority knew about the church in his house,' said John Drummond.

'If the Sheriff wants to start a rebellion, why does he want the help of Spain?' asked Francis.

'It's Spain that wants it that way, to make it easier when the *Armada* arrives, more gold and silver, means the Sheriff can buy more Catholics to fight for their cause.'

'What are we going to do about it then?'

'We buccaneer are on the wrong side of the law always, but the Sheriff is another enemy within. The government should know about it. I'll inform a parliament member that I have uncovered the plot. Meanwhile we must go and get De Souza's gold. He is floating around amongst the English fleet, it would be difficult to trace.'

'For that expedition we need two ships. We shall have to get mine ready. I'll go for him first then you came from the back.'

Within the next few days both buccaneer and their men were busy working on Francis ship. The rudder broken from the last journey was repaired, and the ship was sailable once more. Canons were fitted on like before, gunpowder barrels all lined up, boars and arrows and cutlasses were at hand. The journey would be precarious in challenging both the rough seas and finding out the right vessel to strike amidst the many English flags on the ships they would come across. De Souza's ship, being camouflaged with the utmost deception, was no different. Apart from the flag his ship carried, he got a figurehead that looked very much English. To aim for her could present a headache for both John and Francis. But Coldicot, far from being a weak man had recovered enough from his ordeal of being lashed a few times, could be the man to identify the ship that captured him.

Before both buccaneers were ready for the expedition, none of the crew was allowed out on the shore. It was the only way not to let words inadvertently travelled across on land.

Coldicot was released from the stake but his hands still tied. He was constantly under the watchful eye of the crew. He knew any false move would result in his renewed torture. He might as well toe the line. He had to make sure which was the right ship, must not try to get killed but couldn't care less about *The Conqueror* and her crew, nor the Colonel and Pedro. He was a schemer, ready to appropriate all the gold for himself, hidden away in Hispaniola. Although John Drummund got the map, Coldicot seemed to possess a photographic memory of the spot where to dig out. He hoped things would work out as planned; meanwhile he had to get to Hispaniola safe and alone, manipulated his way, and tried to get out of *The Conqueror,* alive.

The day had arrived to set sail. Both John Drummund and Francis Hopkins had fully prepared their own vessels. The aim was to capture, or destroy the Colonel ship for the gold. They knew the battle would be cruel, with inevitable loss of lives. Coldicot was to travel along with John, and Francis got his own crew. Both vessels had to be closed to each other, but Francis would bring up the rear.

After they bid farewell and good luck, they exchanged a few words:

'Come back safe. Remember we have to capture that Colonel alive as far as possible. He is the proof of the Sheriff underhand dealings,' said John.

'What about Coldicot?' asked Francis.

'We have to keep him safe too!' replied John.

They soon departed their separate ways afterwards.

The weather was hot, but the sea was rough. The waves constantly billowed, like storm in a tea cup. All the ships, bearing English flags, the Colonel's among them were racing one way only: the strong winds were in command. Ships had to move fast, aware of the directions they were going in case they bumped into each other. But to be in control wasn't that easy. Ahead, *The Conqueror* was leading the way, followed by *The Pelican*, Francis ship. The waves were mountain high in places. The sails were being blown like balloons, some torn with the ferocious display of the wind savagery, leaving ships somewhat out of control. As a result some ploughed into each other. One came very close to *The Conqueror,* but John only managed to steer away, by giving her a wide berth. It was a Spanish vessel!

'That's him, Sire, that's him,' shouted Coldicot aboard *The Conqueror*, standing by the captain.

It was Colonel De Souza who was steering dangerously with another skipper by his side, moving fast ahead. But John had already swapped the main English flag for that of a Spanish one. This subterfuge seemed to have worked out well. But the Colonel had his suspicion, as he desperately wanted to know who was aboard *The Conqueror.*

The three ships now were near the Spanish waters. Colonel De Souza's ship was leading the way. And the stormy sea showed no sign of a break in its battering.

The *Armada* was in full view. Standing proud and tall, she showed little concern of what went on outside. She only moved with the float, like a sleeping giant ready to cause chaos when disturbed.

'Good Lord that the tallest thing I have ever encountered. I must see what's she is made of. Get the fire ready lads,' said John.

John wanted to upset her peaceful slumbering. He moved closer to see where he could strike. Francis knew his plan, as he had preempted his every move.

The cannons were lit with firing precision to shoot as *The Conqueror* moved closer. Two shots were fired. The *Armada* was shaken with big bruises at the hull. The cannon balls went through like asteroids hitting the earth, with explosive sounds and black smokes. This was more than a shock to the Armada. To the crew on board it must be a living nightmare. They started firing back. But all the shots from the towering *Armada* missed their intended targets, as they could only fire from a certain height, while the smaller vessels underneath did the damage.

Colonel De Souza heard the noise of battle, as he was amongst the ones commanded to guard the huge vessel. He faltered, and then moved closer to see what was going on. He started firing at *The Conqueror*, but missed. *The Pelican* was moving faster to provide cover. Another shot was fired, and *The Conqueror* was hit. The stern and the rudder were smoking badly with sporadic tongs of flames leapt out. Meanwhile Francis arrived with *The Pelican,* constantly firing at the Colonel ship, until all the top sails and Poop Deck were pulverised. Flames had taken over the whole ship now which drove the crew wild with fear. They all tried to jump overboard onto lifeboats, but only a few succeeded.

Both John and Francis didn't want to annihilate the Spanish vessel altogether. They wanted either the Colonel or Pedro alive to present the case of conspiracy to the organised Catholic rebellion in Court. Above all they wanted the possible gold and silver on board. But how to get them alive would be difficult, now that the whole ship was going down in smoke, and the inferno was hell.

Francis managed to get *The Pelican* closer to the sinking ship. The surrounding black smoke was too much for visibility. He had a long look anyway, no sign of life. Everybody must have perished in the raging sea. Instead of searching for the Colonel and his compatriots, he attended to the more pressing need of saving *The Conqueror* as she was still in full view smouldering away.

The *Conqueror* was badly burnt. Captain Drummond had to act quickly to save his ship. The stern was smouldering with clouds of smoke engulfing the whole ship. It was a dangerous mission to investigate at sea level. To repair any damage at the water edge wouldn't be a good idea. John didn't want to risk the life of his crew to go down there. But the one life he wouldn't hesitate to lose was Coldicot, because apart from the man being enigmatic and dangerous, he was thorn aboard the ship. He suddenly realised that Coldicot knew where his treasure was buried in Hispaniola, although the directions were vague. He wished he had shot Coldicot dead now, there and then in the hole he dug, to 'guard' the treasure!

As panic intensified on board, Captain Drummond reacted:

'Go down there Coldicot, try to fix the rudder,' ordered John.

'How am I going to get there Sire?'

'I'll untie you. Quickly go down by the rope ladder. I will be watching you with the gun, therefore don't try to escape.'

Coldicot went rushing down the rope ladder as soon as he was untied. The black smoke engulfing the rear had gone worse. Visibility was nil. But there were no flames. The rear was gradually going down. No sign of Coldicot either, he had vanished in the smoke, nowhere to be found!

But Francis arrived just on time as he went closer to the ill-fated ship. The relief aboard *The Conqueror* were apparent as they all anxiously tried to jump ship. Some jostled, and some completely missed the deck of the closing ship as they landed in the roaring sea. But they still managed to swim courageously only to be rescued with ropes hanging across the deck of *The Pelican*.

The whole crew were eventually safely aboard *The Pelican*. John Drummond was very thankful to Francis, and sad too about losing his own ship as they moved away. But there was some glimmer of hope. The raging storm had abated. When he looked back, *The Conqueror* was still floating, with the rear immersed halfway under water, all smokes had gone. Some essential items could still be retrieved, he thought.

'Let's get back and get the cannons and ammunitions Francis. Perhaps we can save the whole ship too. I know it will be a perilous attempt, we must go before the 'Spanish morons' get there first,' said John.

'I bet those cannons and heavy things were at the sinking edge. If we can get them off, this will steady the ship,' said Francis.

'Good idea...let's get nearer and see what we can do,' said John.

CHAPTER 5

Approaching *The Conqueror*, burning smells of wood carcasses wafted the site. The smell wouldn't go away it seemed. It became worse with the crackling sound of the loose burnt wood moving recklessly with the waves. But the weather had grown much calmer. They stood nearer to the stricken vessel, watching the waves melting away by degrees. A gentle breeze was now blowing, and John Drummund wasted no time to get on with the hard works ahead.

> 'Get the ropes ready lads. Two of you go there, and tie the ropes round the cannons, while we pull them on board this ship,' ordered John Drummund.

The men managed to get aboard *The Conqueror* despite the fear she was about to disintegrate any moment. The sails were still in place not badly damaged. All the four cannons and ammunitions had slid towards gravity at the rear, congregated. The rudder was partly burnt, so was the stern. The anchor chain was taut under the strain of keeping the ship afloat, and the anchor itself remained fixed, undisturbed, as it was still doing its job in stopping the ship from travelling freely in the wind.

Ropes were wrapped round the cannons, and they were pulled one by one onto the other ship. The weighty cannonballs and boxes were being lifted next and carried away. They were nearly done when the rear popped up with the sound of displaced water. John Drummund breathed a sigh of relief, as he looked at Francis. He went aboard and saw that the anchor had disengaged itself from where it was lodged. He managed to pull it back despite the chain showing sign of giving way. He knew then that there was still hope in saving the whole ship.

Captain Drummond was fortunate that the wind was blowing in his favour, but food supplies were running low. They had to bear home to recuperate.

'I'll take over my ship again, you can carry on Francis. I must hurry whilst the wind is on our side,' said John.

'I think you'll be fine if you rearrange the sails a bit. And where are you off to?' asked Francis.

'To England...got no choice. You better bear that way too. I'll take a couple of mates with me to fix the ship. See you anon. Will you follow me at the back?' asked John.

'I think I will. No hope of going further north, too risky, one day I'll do it,' replied Francis.

Whilst preparing to depart, a distant boat attracted John's attention. A galleon appeared lost, moving erratically and aimlessly.

'Look, there is boat out there. She is trying to get away now. Go and get her, while I careered on,' said John.

Francis had a long look; indeed, a galleon was circling round and round, stuck.

He gathered his crew around and told them about his next move.

'Ahoy, get ready lads, let's go after that boat there...We shall be back soon John, watch us from behind,' continued Francis.

Francis turned his ship round, although the wind direction was blowing the other way. The sea was peaceful unlike the rage before. His ship was moving as expected with its sails well organised. The distant galleon on the other side was having problems, fighting its way, with its sails all over the place. She loitered, heading somewhere but ended nowhere. It seemed there was nobody on board, like a ghost ship. But Francis had to approach her with care, in case it was a trap.

The strategy he used would be worth a try. Instead of started firing recklessly, a lifeboat fully equipped with ropes, pistols, cutlasses and two skippers on board was the solution. This was a bold attempt by Francis despite the risk. But he had to keep them cover all the way, although he knew the extra firing power of *The Pelican* would be outstanding against that flimsy galleon.

He found two reliable coxswains among the crew for the renewed expedition.

'You two fellows get that boat out there before we lost her. Throw the ropes over deck and climb up. See if there is anybody on board,' ordered Francis.

The two skippers rowed the lifeboat fast enough to catch up with the galleon. They approached her silently and furtively. Up they threw the ropes. They reached the deck, and immediately started searching: two skippers lying flat on the deck, no sign of life. They were badly soaked, and dead. They looked foreign. But there was somebody moving, and breathing when they looked further. Although hopelessly worn out, dejected, and soaked they made sure he was disarmed. They instantly removed the wet pistol on him, accosted him with guns and cutlasses.

'Can you speak English?' asked one of the pirates, pointing a gun at him.

'A little bit Signor, don't shoot, don't shoot,' begged the man.

One of the pirates stood by him with the gun, while the other signalled to Francis to berth by the side.

Francis along with more pirates entered the galleon, took no notice of the two dead men as he went straight to the one alive.

'What is your name?' asked Francis.

'Pedro.'

'I have heard that name before. What's happen to the other men? You killed them?'

'No Signor, I saw them swimming, trying to climb ship.'

'Did you see the ship on fire?'

'Yes, Signor, but arrived too late. Weather too bad.'

'What were you doing with the ship on your own?'

'When I see ship on fire, I came to save Colonel and his men, Signor, but too late.'

Pedro sat down at floor level with his back resting on a barrel. Captain Francis studied him closely, with his eyes constantly on him. He desperately wanted to know what that person was up to alone on a galleon, with two dead men on board.

With a pistol in his hand, he asked his men to watch Pedro while he searched every corner of the vessel. He went inside a bunker by climbing down a ladder. The light was minimal, but still managed to detect, shockingly a wooden chest, hermetically sealed underneath some sails. He didn't know what was inside. It appeared heavy.

He shouted from the bunker:

'Ahoy, out there I need some help ….'

Two more men suddenly appeared. Francis showed them what to do:

'Carry that chest on to the main ship. Then come back here,' he ordered.

The pirates did as they were told. When they arrived back, he had other orders to give:

'Throw these two dead men overboard. They have no use for us. And take this man, whatever his name is, onto our ship. When you come back, take over this ship, to Plymouth we bear. I'll follow you at the rear.'

CHAPTER 6

Aboard *The Pelican*, Pedro recovered well from his exhaustion and anguish. He was given dried clothing to wear, but being kept as a prisoner. He would have a lot to talk about, regarding his motives to both John and Francis. As he sat down with hands and feet tied up, under the watchful eyes of the pirates, he knew his life was under threat, with the possibility of walking the plank. What he didn't know was that he had to face the Sheriff of Plymouth sometimes, and the plot concocted, which he was aware of, would amount to treason. But he had to face John Drummund first who could be ruthless in trying to get words out of him: He was between the devil and the deep blue sea, but the devils were everywhere for him!

On the long journey back, the sea remained calm, the wind continued to blow in the right direction for them. Francis ships managed to catch up with *The Conqueror*, although she remained some distance away, but they finally reached Plymouth. There were some extra ships at the harbour, all congregated, engaging in lots of activities, people rushing here and there: They were indeed preparing for war. Coast guards with guns and swords were going around in groups, watching the coast closely, advising everybody around what to do because the *Armada* was on her way.

One of the guards approached John Drummund:

'The *Armada* is on the way Sir. Her Majesty advised people to take shelter, or prepare to defend if they can. We are recruiting people. If you and your men are kind enough to offer assistance the Queen will greatly appreciate.'

Showing the carbonized rear of his ship, John Drummond said:

'I have to see to my ship first Sir before I can offer help.'

'This won't do Sir; the Spaniards will be here tonight. Your ship like the others would surely take the onslaught anyway.'

The guards seemed adamant in their beliefs that Spain would invade on the night. To contradict that claim could lead to unnecessary arguments resulting in imprisonment for John. But he knew full well about the impossibility of the *Armada* reaching the English soil sooner, because of the damages he, and the other pirates inflicted on the Armada a few days ago. The Armada would take some time to recover from the deep holes at the hulls and burning at the stern.

John kept his cool, said nothing, and walked away.

The other buccaneers soon arrived and berthed nearby. Francis and his men were met with the same boring news by the coast guards, which they derided.

There was hardly anybody by the coast. At the nearby villages, the daily activities of the peasants were broken with the news of the impending war. Some were running wild, eager to take some sort of shelter, many went in hiding.

Francis soon met up with John:

> 'What are you going to do with that Pedro then? I got him on board with me. I got a wooden chest, and his ship too,' said Francis.

> 'What! You got his ship and his chest too. I can't believe it. Good of you cousin, I know you are invincible, but not to that extent!' said John Drummond

John spent no time to get back on Francis ship, *The Pelican*. On board he came across Pedro tied to a mast, he took less notice of him. He was more interested to see the wooden chest first. It was left out of sight in the Captain office.

As the chest was fastened tight with padlock, both pirates had to use iron bar and iron mallet to break the lock. The lid at last was free. What both pirates saw was enough to make them faint: It was half full of gold bullions!

'I think we shall have to take that away quickly to our apartment Francis to look through. Can you go and fetch a coach, there is nobody on board I think apart from this man. I'll question him, while you are away. He may tell me something about Coldicot. I think he is still alive somewhere!' said John.

'You sure you'll be ok, because the man is dangerous. I don't know how much Coldicot told him about your hidden treasure in Hispaniola. He may tell lies, tries to get away. Can't you wait till I get back?'

'Ok...I will.'

Despite John Drummond agreed not to approach Pedro, he couldn't resist the temptation not to talk to the man, who had grown thinner by degrees, due to the malnourishment on board.

Pedro still possessed that ferocity in his devious character, a certain diehard attitude not to get killed. He had kept wriggling with the tight rope on him since the ship berthed, but only just managed to get out of it when both John and Francis appeared. It was indeed frustrated for him. Were it a little earlier, he could have escaped with everything!

Captain John Drummond approached Pedro at the mast fully armed, cutlass in one hand, pistol in the other, and started the questioning. Pedro was standing with hands and feet tied to the mast, subdued looking, very much alive. But the loose ropes on him, had hoodwinked John Drummond into thinking that Pedro was securely tied.

'Where were you going with that boat alone, then?'

Pedro didn't answer. He looked wild with fear at Captain Drummond.

The sword was pointing at his throat now, and sweats were forming rapidly on his face like he was on fire at the stake.

Captain Drummond started to grow impatient. He wouldn't hesitate to bruise his neck if he remained mute.

He again asked:

'Where is Coldicot?'

As soon as Coldicot's name was mentioned, indiscriminate shouts were heard, loud enough to distract Captain Drummond. It was those Town Criers again. They were going round delivering more messages of the imminent dangers about the invasion. Sound of horses running wild, neighing and galloping outside, were deafening.

The Captain was stunned. He turned his head quickly towards the noise, but it was a big mistake. Pedro knew too well that was the best chance of his life to strike, as he was already free from the ropes, which was only resting, seemingly tied on him.

He quickly took a swipe at the sword pointing at him, and kicked the hand holding the gun. The bullet went off target, as the gun was accidentally triggered with the impact. The hand lost its grip, and the gun landed on the floor. Captain Drummond shockingly flinched, instantly picked the gun up, and took a shot at the runaway Spaniard, but missed.

Two equestrian guards on the road heard the shot. They were intrigued, desperately wanted to know where it came from. Their eyes searched everywhere.

A coach was approaching at the same time, the guards stopped it. It was Francis.

'Have you seen anything suspicious, Sir,' asked one of the guards.

'I saw a man running wild in the opposite direction Sir… Seize him quick. He may be a Spanish spy,' said Francis.

One of the guards gave chase, while the other one stood behind, wanted to know what Francis was up to.

'Can I have a look inside your coach Sir?' the guard asked.

'You may Sir you'll find nothing. Both my friend and I had just arrived from the sea. I've got a carriage to carry our things since we aren't allowed to stay on board.'

The guard searched the coach. He accompanied Francis towards *The Pelican* afterwards. But John Drummond saw them coming, he didn't want the guard to come on board the ship. He went to meet them halfway instead.

'I heard a shot coming from your side Sir. Have you seen anything?' asked the guard.

'Yes, it was a Spanish spy Sir. He was trying to kill me but missed. He ran away when he heard the horses. Go after him. He may bear towards the Sheriff house,' said John Drummond.

'And why the Sheriff, Sir?' asked the guard.

'How well do you know the Sheriff Sir?... I guess you should be aware about the Sheriff conspiracy. He is part of a plot to start a Catholic uprising during the *Armada* invasion. They won't believe you perhaps about this piece of information, because the Sheriff is too eminent a man to do such a thing. But it's the truth. Now that you know about, you should watch your back, they may come after you.'

'I don't work for the Sheriff Sir I work for the Inquisition.'

'I thought Her Majesty is against the use of Inquisition!'

'Yes, she does Sir, although she has moderate views. But with the *Armada* coming we must search houses for Catholic dissident priests. It's them who are the problem, they are helping Spain.'

'Well said Sir. I think you should go to the Sheriff house then before it's too late. I can assure you the *Armada* is not coming tonight, nor tomorrow, or the next day, because my cousin and I did some serious damage to it. I am going to contact the Government Spy Catcher now, after we transfer everything from here onto our carriage.'

'You do that Sir, while I go after that man.'

As the guard left, John Drummond still shocked from his lack of foresight resulted in Pedro's escape. Francis couldn't believe that the man managed to wriggle out from the tight rope. Instead of brooding over what happened and argued, they both quickly transferred the treasure chest onto the coach.

They sat side by side, holding on to the rein at the front of the coach, while on their way to John's apartment.

They couldn't stop thinking of Pedro on the loose. Being so unpredictable and dangerous, he could be lurking anywhere, before he reached the Sheriff abode.

All the way they were met with renewed calls through the cone loudspeakers, telling people that the *Armada* wouldn't be coming on the night. That people could rest in peace.

Despite the long hot summer's day and the big relief, hardly any soul was around. The few houses along the way were shut. Only smokes were belching out of their chimneys. But when they reached a pool across the road, the scene was different. Few folks were swimming, and some women folk were doing washing in a separate pond further down the road. Bread and honey sellers in a coach were here too.

Both buccaneers stopped to have something to eat and drink, and to inquire about the fugitive. John asked one of the bread sellers:

'Did you see anybody foreign here Sir.'

'I surely did Sir, and a thief too.'

'Was he wild, with any weapon?' asked Francis.

'He was rough, holding a wooden club Sir. He grabs some of my bread and run away with it,' said the bread seller.

'Couldn't you fight him off, or gun him down?' asked John.

'No Sir. I am on my own. I don't possess a gun,' replied the bread seller.

'Do you know which direction he went?' asked John.

'Along the road and disappeared inside the bush.'

Both buccaneers were shocked to hear about the dangerous man. Once they were on the road again, they were forever on the look-out for anything suspicious in the bushy hedge rows. But they were still puzzled by the sudden news about the *Armada*.

'How did they know now the Armada is not coming? I am sure Pedro must have arrived at the Sheriff to tell him what happened,' said John Drummond.

'Not necessarily. It could be one of the guards too. Remember Pedro is on foot. He couldn't possibly have covered the long distance from here,' replied Francis.

'You'll be surprised what a fugitive could do. Wait, stop! I saw a man trying to get inside that bush. I am sure it's he,' said John.

'Somebody is trying to relieve himself more than likely!' replied Francis.

'Possible, but I am sure it's he. You wait here with your gun, watching. I go after him with my pistol. Don't hesitate to shoot him down when you see him around,' said John.

John went out quickly with his gun as soon as they stopped the coach and heading straight to where he saw the man. He got no trail to follow, only the marked territory by the pong left behind, not necessarily Pedro though!

He started to search everywhere near. He heard something ruffled, he took a shot. A wild boar ran out screeching with pain.

John didn't want to proceed any further, in case he got lost in this dense and ancient woodland. He had a look around, from side to side. He heard indiscriminate shootings nearby. His insecurity and fear for his life started to grow. He got out of the woods, quickly ran towards the coach.

Francis was waiting anxiously by the coach, with guns in both hands.

'Have you seen, or heard anything? I heard some gun shots, I thought you were having problems!' said John.

'I heard the same. I think it came further down the road. We better go and drop our bounty home before being ambushed.'

En route, reaching a crossroad, they heard the sound of another coach approaching. They stopped. They found two guards at the front, holding on to the reins, and another two at the back with guns, watching somebody inside a carriage, what looked like a wooden railings cage, being towed. The cage was a provisional mobile prison to carry prisoners, like wild animals, to a more secure prison.

John made signs for the coach to stop as he got down from his own, and went to meet the guards.

Both buccaneers recognised the guards at the front. They were the same ones they met before.

'May I have a look at your prisoner Sir,' he asked.

'You may Sir, he is hurt in the arm, but not serious,' replied one of the guards.

John had a look through. The prisoner was sitting down, leaning against the wall of the cage, exhausted and rough, eyes wide-opened. It was Pedro, with blood stains on his dirty white shirt.

He didn't hesitate to ask him again:

'What happened to Coldicot then?'

Worn out and exhausted Pedro knew at that point he had nothing to gain, or to lose. He would surely end up in the gallows anyway, no chance of getting hold of Captain John Drummond's hidden treasure in Hispaniola. He might as well tell the Captain what he knew.

'I saw him hanging on to a plank in the high wave, trying to reach my boat, but I have to save the Colonel first,' said Pedro.

'And did you?' asked the Captain.

'Too late Signor, the Colonel went down the sea, dead. Two of his men reached me, but they too died on board,' said Pedro.

'Where were you going on your own with that boat?' asked the Captain.

'We were all guarding the *Armada*. When I saw Colonel ship on fire, I went to help,' said Pedro.

'You and the Colonel were on your way to see the Sheriff when the *Armada* was struck?' continued the Captain.

'Yes Signor!'

As John was talking, the guards were growing impatient, and dusk was looming. They have to move on, heading for the secure prison at the Sheriff, where he held the key. Otherwise the prisoner had to be guarded on overnight watch in his cage, which could be dangerous.

But the Sheriff lived upstairs in the same location, where he secretly practiced his religion. Nobody got access to it even his guards if they weren't Catholics. All well-known personnel allowed had to be accompanied by him. He normally employed guards to stay downstairs when there was somebody locked up.

Being a Catholic priest, he led a double life. Not even his guards knew of his Catholicism and dark motives. Even if they knew, it was a big secret!

He knew all about Coldicot though as the latter was locked up for minor offences in the past when he arrived from Ireland to seek his fortune. Owing to his Catholic affiliation, Coldicot was reprieved on compassionate grounds, and given employment to work in the Sheriff stable. But he soon realised his mistakes, as he started to grow suspicious of Coldicot especially during

Colonel de Souza's visit. He desperately wanted to 'get rid' of Coldicot, who felt being unwanted, with his life in danger.

The Sheriff knew that Coldicot had joined the pirates where Captain Drummond and his sea adventures were held highly by Her Majesty's government. Any attempts on Coldicot's life could be dangerous if found, as his undercover religious plot could be revealed.

He never dreamt to see Coldicot again, as the life expectancy of a pirate was short indeed. He couldn't believe his eyes when he saw Coldicot in Spanish hands, arrived with gold, and being given a better status.

CHAPTER 9

The Sheriff and a guard had just arrived back on his coach and horses. When the *posse* (Inquisition) stopped by, both he and his guard weren't there. But his coach was outside, where the two horses were nibbling the grasses on the ground. They both seemed to have disappeared as they could sense danger, while watching the *posse* arriving. They stealthily went through the backdoor to reach upstairs.

The Sheriff got no power over the Inquisition at the time. They were an independent group seconded by the Queen's secretary to go around and searched for Catholic dissidents who wanted to overthrow Elizabeth the First to replace her with a Catholic heir.

The Inquisition was a law into themselves. They would tract down any known dissidents in houses, forcibly removed them from locked rooms, and tortured them until they confessed to their crimes.

It was a big surprise to see the Sheriff location all locked up, despite his coach and horses were outside. But the Inquisition guards knew the Sheriff was inside. After a long wait, two guards came down their horses, repeatedly hammered on the door. At last his guard arrived to open the door, very frightened.

'Where is the Sheriff Sir? I have brought a Spanish prisoner here,' said the guard from the Inquisition.

'The Sheriff is not here Sir,' said the Sheriff's guard.

'May we ask you to find him?'

The Sheriff guard went silent, while he stood at the doorway anxious, with terror in his eyes. The two guards from the Inquisition forced their way inside. They communed among themselves, bearing in mind what they knew about the Sheriff. They couldn't care about his religious affiliation, but the use of his religion to assist Catholic dissidents to overthrow the monarchy was treason. They had to find him by all means!

'Is he anywhere here Sir,' repeated the guards.

'He is not upstairs. I had a look earlier,' replied the guard, showing some restlessness as he couldn't stand still.

'In this case we shall have to go and have a look ourselves Sir, with you coming with us.'

They disarmed the guard first, and all three went up the squeaky stairs, with the Sheriff guard leading the way.

There were two big rooms, but one of them was his bedroom. The other was like a chapel, furnished with some wood benches, a table contained a bible and a wooden sculptured of Jesus Christ nailed to a cross, standing between two lit candles.

The candles were the only source of light, where their ghostly shadows projected on the wall moved as they walked around.

They searched the big bedroom next, under the bed, inside the wardrobe, and under any loose floorboard. They found nobody. They then went back into the Chapel room, searched everywhere in a similar fashion. They asked the guard again, but this time they had a sword pointing to his throat:

'Where is he hiding Sir?'

'I don't know Sir, perhaps he went out through the window!' said the guard.

They went by the windows, had a look through. They were too high and small for him to go through. They heard a squeak behind a large picture frame hanging on the wall, which could be well mistaken for a mouse. But one of the guards went by the picture, taking a lit candle with him, tried to investigate. The frame appeared to move as he held it, and suddenly the whole picture fell down with a bang. They were all shocked by the noise, but there was something else on the wall behind that picture: a longish piece of varnished wood, well camouflaged with the wall. It seemed that the guards had seen it all before: that there was somebody hiding inside that wall.

They removed the camouflaged wood, which slot into the wall frame. Within the narrow opening, the lit candle was held there.

The Sheriff was lying on the floor in the narrow space. Both guards with swords ready for action, watching him coming out, as he was disarmed.

'We arrest you Sir in the name of Her Majesty for conspiracy with the Catholics to bring down the Crown,' said the guard.

'You can't arrest me Sir, I am the Sheriff, employed by her Majesty, and a judge for this Town,' said the Sheriff.

'We are aware of this Sir, but you will have to explain yourself at the Bloody Tower. We had one of your Spanish colleagues with us!' said the guard.

They immediately tied his hands at the back, led him inside the wooden prison cage of the carriage to join Pedro, but they left his guard behind as they suspected his innocence.

On their way out, they were met again by John Drummond, and Francis Hopkins, who had just disposed their valuable possessions. They came back to see if Pedro was locked up. They both got down their carriage to inquire:

'So, you've got the Sheriff too Sir. It's no surprise you find him. I heard so many stories about him disappearing in the background,' said John Drummond.

'He indeed vanished Sir, but we knew where to find him,' replied one of the guards.

'Where are you taking them now?' asked John.

'To London, not to see the Queen though, but the Bloody Tower, where they will pay for their crimes. They will be 'drawn and quartered' like many others of their kind,' replied the guard

He continued:

'Will you be kind enough to look after this place for us during our absence, Sir? His assistant got the key. It would be a long journey ahead of us travelling to London with our prisoners, and had to make it an overnight journey. '

'Ok Sir, off you go. We shall stay here, till you get back,' said John Drummond.

The Inquisition cortege moved on as the guards had to change a few horses and buffeted on the way. But they were prepared for all the mishaps of being ambushed in the dark country lanes. With their guns and swords ready, they had to move faster, and with trepidation.

John Drummond and Francis Hopkins moved in the Sheriff apartment. Even though they were buccaneers, they were imbued with that sense of nationalism, ready to defend the country. They knew their livelihood in both land and sea was at stake, and had to keep Spain away by all means, although they were no men of religion!

Printed in Poland
by Amazon Fulfillment
Poland Sp. z o.o., Wrocław

54573590R00058